I0726237

www.powderriverpublishing.com

The Italian's Duty-Bound Bride

Published by:
Powder River Publishing LLC
1014 Black Mountain Road
Thermopolis, Wyoming 82443

Copyright © 2022
ISBN: 978-1-956881-23-3
Printed in the United States of America

Table of Contents

Chapter 1

He held her tight.

Santo Barrella squeezed his dying Nonna's shoulders. Maddie Adams stood hesitantly in the dimness inside the door. The kaleidoscope of emotions zipping across his profile was heartrending. The urge to comfort him threatened to overtake her. It had been a long time.

She'd spent the last two years trying to forget him. She thought she'd succeeded but had only been fooling herself. Now, confronted with his hot, frightfully gorgeous image her frazzled nerves were taut with panic. The rapid pounding of her heart resonated in her ears.

"What are you doing here?" a pained, deep voice snapped from within the shadows lurking around the bed.

Maddie froze. The deep husky timbre of his voice skidded across her already over-sensitive skin sending shock waves through her sensory nerves. Nothing could calm the rapid flutter of her increased heartbeat. Her breath lodged in her throat. The truth was the weeks, the months, of pain mysteriously crystallized again. She'd spent the past twenty-four months building a rigid barrier around her heart but hearing his voice made it all come crashing down.

He rose from the edge of the bed and stepped into the light. He looked tired and haggard. His hair was mussed like he hadn't slept. But his super seismic persona hadn't lessened. Increased saliva moistened her tongue and piercing arrows of sensation darted along her torso. The breath she'd been holding whooshed from her lungs.

He was as handsome as ever. The years hadn't changed that. His metallic grey eyes sizzled with electrified energy honed in on her wan, ashen face. She took a careful breath. Even under immense pressure the man was devastating. His powerful body, broad width of his shoulders and, leanness of his waist was made more intimidating by the shadows surrounding him. The hitch in his voice was gruff and not the least bit happy. But, why should it be?

Their parting hadn't been civil or cordial. He hated her, resented her. Blamed her.

Cautiously, she stepped into his direct line of vision. She moved silently and softly as to not disturb Nonna. His grandmother's willow thin form was covered with the stark white sheets. Her eyes were closed, and her skin ashen gray. Shock filled Maddie. She hadn't expected to find the once spry patriarch nearly diminished to nothing. Tears burned beneath her lashes.

"I love Nonna too," she said simply.

Their gazes clashed and collided.

His resentful gleam locked on her face sending sharp laser beams slicing through her body. She raised her head her tender doe like eyes pleading for his understanding.

His firm lips lifted in a snarl of condemnation. He moved toward her, standing, dwarfing over her. "Isn't it a bit late for that?"

A dull headache throbbed behind her tired eyes. She stood her ground planting her feet firmly against the tiled floor. Not backing down from his domineering presence. You dare not show weakness before the master tactician or you'd become his prey. Santo was famous for pouncing on the weak to hone his successful business portfolio.

"I," she paused, "uh, have this." She held out a white envelope. "It came a while ago. I debated rather to come or not. But I had to." His fingers brushed hers as he grasped the paper. The awareness was ever present. She jerked her hand away, shocked by her fiery response. Distance hadn't stopped that. "Nonna wrote it. She wanted me here."

He glanced at the tattered envelope. Her fingers clamped the paper in a death grip. Seconds, moments ticked by. His predatory gaze locked and held hers. "She shouldn't have," he stated finally. "I don't want you here. It's personal and private, and you are no longer a part of it."

His words sliced through her. It hurt, even now, two years later. His uncanny ability to destroy her firmly held within his grasp. Her gaze fell onto his lips, firm lips, kissable lips. She closed her eyes shielding the rippling awareness that entered them. The memory of those lips upon hers still rattled her. He'd been her world, her rock, before it had crumbled. She must put a stopper on the instantaneous attraction. It would never do. She was here for Nonna, nothing more.

His lips quirked knowingly. His cool grey eyes reflected the knowledge that he knew the effect he still had on her. A fiery blush rose up her neck. She resented his ability to make her feel helpless and needy. Humiliation splashed over her. Heat blazed onto her cheeks.

His steel eyes narrowed into slits. "You should catch the next flight home, Maddie. I'll handle this."

"No!" They both turned toward the faint voice. A frown creased his brow. "No, Santo, she stays." Nonna vehemently demanded, even in her weakened, frail condition.

Santo rushed back to his grandmother's side. Clasping her fragile, veined hand, he whispered, "Don't worry, Nonnina, lay back and rest."

"My rest will be eternal soon, Santo. And if I

want the people closest to me by my side then so be it."

"But," she stopped him mid-sentence. Pressing her finger to his lips she sighed, "No, moroso, Maddie stays." She motioned for Maddie to take her other hand.

Maddie promptly laced their fingers together. Tears trickled down her cheeks.

"Don't cry for me, my dear, my pain and suffering are great. I've had a good life." She squeezed each of their hands. "What I want is for the people I love to be happy. Embrace life. Forgiveness is a wonderful thing," she smiled weakly.

• • •

The next few days were a haze. Santo withdrew into himself. She didn't try to console him. His grizzled appearance and short fused attitude were unapproachable. He handled all the funeral arrangements while completely ignoring her presence. There was no calm after the storm. Things should've quietened down after the funeral.

She felt isolated and alone.

Maddie was numb inside. She drank a lot of black coffee. She chewed on her nails biting off every last bit of their polished surface. She strolled around the perfectly manicured gardens surrounding the villa. She cursed Santo under her breath for causing a resurgence of mixed emotions.

Many tears fell for Nonna, what-ifs, what-might-have-been, and the unanswered questions of Maddie's bleak future.

The day of the funeral service gray ominous clouds rolled in, and a light mist of rain began to fall. A small crowd attended the service in the quaint chapel on the hill. Maddie kept to the back of the church. Santo greeted those in attendance with a handshake and a smile. Only Maddie knew it was forced, and he was grief-stricken inside. Yet, he valued his privacy.

Nonna was laid to rest beside her husband, her son, and daughter-in-law, who were Santo's parents. As the small crowd dissipated Maddie remained several yards back to allow Santo the opportunity to say his final goodbyes. Maddie's black heels sunk into the moist earth, and her elaborate upswept hairdo became unruly in the moist, humid air. She kept shifting to prevent her six-inch heels from being completely buried in the muck.

Maddie tugged the raincoat closer around her as the drizzle continued to fall. Moisture glistened upon Santo's broad shoulders and down bent head. Her nerves screamed and grief gripped her lower stomach. She commiserated with him. Her sorrow-stricken expression mirrored his.

When he looked up she caught the dreadful sadness that filled his eyes. But then, he stood tall, took a deep breath, and walked straight past her to the waiting vehicle. His rude dismissal hurt. She took a careful breath and forced herself to follow.

The tension was deafening. The return trip to the villa was cast in sorrow. Maddie had ridden with Santo, but he had not spoken. His firm lips remained stiff and firm. He didn't smile nor look her way. Her erratic vein pulsed in her neck as she gallantly tried to respect his grief.

The friction was forever present.

When they arrived home, she cast him a concerned glance. She wanted to comfort him but didn't know how. "Santo, I'm sorry. I know how much you loved Nonna, but you must eat. How many days has it been?"

"My eating habits aren't your concern." He looked at her intently, icy distain upon his face. "You're not my wife anymore, except in name."

The guilt sliced through her like a knife. She could argue that she was, but it'd be a moot point. She turned, ready to run. Run away from the misery of being near him. Her escape was so close, yet so far away.

She could put distance between them, but she couldn't run from her thoughts and mind. Angered heat blazed on her cheekbones. Then to her amazement, he lifted a hand and tucked his forefinger under her chin. He tilted her head. She froze, stunned by the immensity of her response to his slightest touch.

"Did you truly come for Nonna," he threw at her sharply, "or for the Barrella fortune?"

Maddie's face blanched of all color. "How dare you say that to me? I've never wanted anything from you, much less your money."

"There was a time," he stared her down, "when you wanted a lot from me."

Heat scorched her belly sending flaming sparks straight to her center. She knew what he meant. Their intimacy had been magical, unstoppable and so freely given. She wanted to deny it, but it would be a lie. She'd been mesmerized from the first moment they'd touched. He had cast his web around her capturing her in it. She been stunned. And completely and utterly out of her depth of expertise. He was an expert lover. She hadn't returned for this, but his dangerous and dynamic seductive powers were methodically reeling her in.

Instead of boldly challenging him she bowed her head, the blond curtain of her hair falling forward hiding her face. "Those days are gone. We can't bring them back."

"No, we can't," he quickly agreed. The cynical note in voice blunt and direct.

"I'll be gone tomorrow." Maddie promised. "You won't hear from me again, Santo, but we must officially end this. We must get divorced."

"No," he cast out vehemently. "We've discussed that enough. I won't grant a divorce." He sounded annoyed.

She resisted the urge to lash out. The involuntarily flick of her tongue moistened her dry lips. She swept her hand around her neck rubbing the stiff, tense muscles.

"What would you have us do?" She asked softly.   "Stay married and live apart forever?"

"Why not?" His sharp, stormy gray gaze landed on her. He focused on her mouth. The heated gaze compelling her to agree. "The last two years hasn't stopped you from doing what you want."

"Really," she gasped. "You're going to condemn me for continuing my life. As if you put a stop to yours. The tabloids indicated otherwise. There was spread after spread of your amorous exploits."

"That's none of your business!" The cynical edge of his voice dripped with distain.

"But mine is yours?" she countered. "I don't owe you any explanations either, Santo."

The tension in the air was tumultuous. Her

stress meter was skyrocketing. She had hoped the years had softened him, but he was even more intense. She forced out a strained laugh and walked past him to the bank of windows overlooking the lush, rain drenched valley before her. The villa sat within the serene landscape. It had always been her favorite place to be. The apartment in Florence had been too modern and sophisticated for her. She had simple tastes. She loved the countryside.

He came and stood beside her. His nearness made her uneasy. His brows drew together in a formidable crease. "I know, Maddie, that Nonna brought you here." She fixated on his sensual lips. "I respect her wishes, but now that she's gone, you must go. Our lives are no longer connected." His look challenged her to deny it. "You've got yours, and I've got mine. Simple."

What in the world did he expect from her? His excruciating closeness and the warmth of his breath so near her was torture. She lifted her hand and toyed with the loose tendril of hair. She wanted to scream her outrage and kick off her spiked heels and run as fast as her feet would allow. While a much more basic instinct, had her longing to throw her arms around him, and let the heat of his body consume her.

"Not so simple," she shook her head and gently disagreed, "I still want you."

His mouth dropped open with surprise. She heard his swift intake of breath. He didn't know what he'd been expecting, but not that.

Quietness settled between them. She didn't dare look away. She wasn't going to back down, deny what was evident, nor give up without a fight.

Several tense insane minutes ticked past. Finally, he responded. "You're crazy."

She folded her arms across her chest and faced him. She shivered, her gaze bore into his chest. "Don't worry I'm still leaving, but I'm being honest here. We need closure, Santo, real closure, not some made up excuse of why we can't do this anymore."

He continued to stare at her as if she were mad. He raked his fingers through his damp hair. His profile was so intense. His jaw muscle ticked with barely restrained tension. "Nonna's gone we don't need to pretend. I don't love you anymore. I'm not sure I ever did. Our relationship was lust driven Maddie. It was never based upon a solid foundation. And that's why," he continued, "it didn't last."

Redness mounted her cheeks. Fury filled her veins. Why did men always categorize emotions into lust? He had no idea of the personal hell which had consumed her. She wanted to pummel his chest and make him understand. His stoic expression denied the truth. She lifted her eyes that flashed with jealous contempt. "It was based on the fact," she accused him, "that you cheated on me and fathered another woman's child."

He flinched. His jaw clinched, and his knuckles whitened. He glared at her. His belligerent jaw working back and forth with his distress. His eyes filled with the same contempt that she felt. "You still don't know the truth, and it's not worth my time trying to explain it to you."

"Explain what," she cried miserably, "that my husband fell into someone else's bed."
The unfathomable hurt and endless void ached re lentlessly in her veins. She hadn't intended to talk about the past or the monsters that rode her back relentlessly. But his cold, heartless words had shattered her resolve.

"Enough," he snapped forcibly. "I will not be accused of such trash in my own home."

The buried hurt was still unbearable. She couldn't believe she had allowed it to rear its ugly head. "Nonna understood my flight, when you never did," Maddie whispered. She bowed her head feeling defeated.

"Nonna was a romantic," he claimed. "She believed in miracles."

Sadness reflected within his charcoal grey eyes. He loved his grandmother unconditionally. She shook her head sadly. "Most women are, romantics I mean."

His stoic expression was formidable.

"Listen," he said, running his fingers through his already disorderly locks, "I've dealt with enough grief today, and I don't want to discuss our disaster of a marriage." He pursed his lips together with finality.

She eyed his mouth. His perfectly, symmetrical mouth. His kissable mouth. No, she coached herself, don't think about his mouth. The mouth that had brought her so much pleasure, so much joy. She tried to block the image of his sinful lips. She was over him. Over him, she repeated. She mustn't forget how much willpower it had taken to forget him. Change the subject to a safe topic. Food.

She stepped away from him and smoothed her hands over her slender hips. His eyes followed the action lighting their depths. "Then please," she begged, "let me fix you something to eat. Actually, I'm a little famished myself."

He simply nodded.

Maddie recalled Santo never accepted pampering. When they had met three years ago he'd been so driven, so successful, never a moment spent on himself. She'd been a novelty, a distraction.

She'd come to Florence to restore a New York client's Italian villa. They had literally run into each other, of all places, at an antique shop. He'd come through the door, she'd been looking at her list, and they'd collided.

Maddie had been mesmerized from the first moment. His magnetic grey eyes and dark, sultry good looks had captivated her. He was a work of art. He looked like a million bucks and dressed like a million more.

Fate had walked through the door that day, she had lived it, embraced it, and then walked away. And here she stood, two years later, still married to the enigma called a husband.

Maddie shook her head, clearing cobwebs, while he followed her into the kitchen. Focusing on mundane tasks would take her mind off his lethal beauty. "What sounds good?" she asked, while rummaging through the refrigerator.

"Not much," he said, scooping coffee into the maker. "You choose."

She located the ingredients for a simple salad, pasta, and a chilled bottle of Moscato. Placing the food on the table they sat across from each other.

"Coffee?"

She nodded. He filled her cup.

Butterflies fluttered in the pit of her stomach. She was nervous, her palms were sweating, and she nibbled on her lip. The food, she was so hungry for, suddenly tasted like cardboard. She kicked off her heels and placed her aching feet on the cold, tiled floor. She watched him eat. She had married him knowing their relationship was based more on lust than love. He hadn't promised her anything. He'd simply bedded her to appease his hunger. She had convinced herself that desire would be enough, but it hadn't. His infidelity nearly destroyed her. She gave him a pitying look. Frustration filled her.

He looked at her under his lashes, somewhat amused. Any flicker of hope deserted her. He was heartless. Emotions weren't part of his makeup. He neatly practiced logistics. Solving problems with his mind not his heart.

He finished his food, while she'd barely touched hers.

"I thought you were hungry?" He quizzed, leaning back to sip his steaming coffee. He smiled sheepishly. He knew her mind had been racing all over the place. Trying to figure him out. He found humor in all of her frustration. She didn't think it was so funny.

"I guess I wasn't as hungry as I thought," she said, pushing the plate away. She fiddled with the napkin still in her hand.

"Do you want to marry him?" He steepled his fingers next to his chin. A flick of dangerous subtly filled his molten grey eyes.

She flashed him a confused glare. "Who?" she asked. She tried to shift gears, but clarity eluded her. Her mouth opened, then closed.

"Edward Wakefield, the financier." He stared at her daring her to deny it. His gaze converted from self-assured to masked.

"No," she stated adamantly. "He's a colleague and a friend. In case you've forgotten. I'm already married. Wait," she returned his look, suspicious. "How do you know about Edward?"

"I know everything about you, Maddie." The steeliness of his burning eyes penetrated hers. "I've tracked your movements." The bunched muscle, in his jaw, twitched.

Maddie stood. Furious anger filled her veins. Her heart thumbing so heavily that she could hear the annoying pounding in her ear. His ability to irritate her hadn't changed. He had such a cold, ruthless heart. "You've been spying on me?" she spat out. "How dare you?"

The set of his mouth was determined. It broached no argument. His unwavering gaze remained locked on her. His towering height ominous.

"The Barrella name must stay intact," he stated calmly. "I do business all over the world. My reputation is irreputable. Well known in certain circles.

You know that."

     "Seriously," Maddie scowled, pressing the heel of her hand against her breastbone as if it would make her breathe easier. "You've had me watched to protect your integrity? What kind of person do you take me for, Santo?" She lifted her chin, and her long hair tumbled over her shoulder. "I've never done anything to slander your name."

     "You did," he stated calmly. "You walked out on me caro, when I needed you the most."

Chapter 2

Her chest muscles squeezed shut.

Instead of becoming easier her breathing became more difficult. It was no use rehashing dark memories. It didn't serve a purpose. She needed to put a damper on her emotional torment.

Leaving had been difficult at first, but she had healed. Recovery had brought her back to the living, back to her career. Her clientele list was flourishing. She was finally making enough money to live comfortably without worrying how to pay the bills.

Santo was her past, not her future.

He was a powerful man. A world-renowned business magnate. He came from old money but was a risk taker. He had branched out the family business and taken it into the new millennium. He was head of one of the world's leading software companies and listed as one of the wealthiest men alive. He attracted attention everywhere he went. He took the world of high society and high stakes to the next level. A force to be reckoned with. Men envied him, and women adored him. His vision made his prestigious family, very, very wealthy. His conglomerate of businesses was scattered around the globe. Santo's thrill seeking adventurous spirit was limitless.

The jealousy monster had always raised its ugly head when they were together. Maddie never liked that about herself. It wasn't a personality trait she had embraced. She hated it.

Relationships should be based upon trust, loyalty, and love, not distrust.

"I didn't walk out on you," she said, making an exasperated noise. "I had no choice. Our marriage vows were broken, trust gone. What did we have left?"

Her eyes begged him to understand her position.

"You betrayed me," he shot back. "You walked out on our marriage. You left me to make excuses why you weren't here," his voice rang out sharply causing her to flinch.

She felt faint, dizzy. She hadn't expected him to still have this overpowering hold on her emotions.

"How ironic, you accusing me of betrayal."

She had forgotten how he could dominate a room. Her surroundings seemed to vanish in his powerful presence. His anger simmered just beneath the surface. His clenched fists and tense jawline showed his forced restraint. He looked ruthless. She smoothed down her dress. Her palms sweaty. It was no wonder he'd been so innovative in the boardroom.

He sighed, as he put the dishes away. "We've both made mistakes. There's no future in it." He spun around suddenly, "Why do you still want me?"

The question caught her completely off guard. "Uh, uh...," she stammered, "I don't know."

"That's it," his deliberate pause increased the tension in the air. "No further explanation. You want to suck me back into your arms, your web, and take half my fortune. Then laugh in my face?"

"It's not like that. I told you I don't want your money," she answered, her voice breathless and unsteady. "I just thought..."

"Thought what, Maddie?" He stepped forward. He towered over her, alarmingly demanding. A cold, relentless fury on his face.

She meant to step back but couldn't. She froze.

His fingers clamped her shoulders and pulled her forward. The magnetic force was too great. She complied.

"Is this what you thought," he demanded, his mouth reaching hers, "that you would tempt me with your charms."

His mouth found hers. The contact was explosive. Their chemistry had always been powerful, fiery. Her immunity vanished with just one kiss. All their time together came flooding back. The memory of his smile. The memory of his kiss. The memory of their bodies tangled together intimately entwined.

Santo was unprepared for the sudden wave of carnal lust that washed over him. He jerked back.

Maddie wobbled on her feet. She was dazed. How could he have this power over her emotions after all these years? He was lethal. He was a poison to her system. The only cure was separation and distance. Then she could cope. But here in his arms it all vanished. His magnetism was as powerful force pulling her under his spell. She pulled away and touched her tingling lips. Dazed confusion sweltered within her eyes.

His face darkened, confusion evident. "You need to leave, Maddie. Tonight, not tomorrow. I'll think this divorce thing over."

And just like that he was dismissing her from his life. Like she was a business deal gone bad. She looked at him. The finality was clear. The hurt swamped her yet again. Santo was the one person in life she was destined to love forever but couldn't live with. After all the glorious days spent in his arms he was still distant and withdrawn.

Maybe it was time she gave Edward a chance. Edward treated her with care and precision. He was gentle and kind catering to her slightest wish. The torch she'd been carrying for her husband was finally burning out. For him anyway. She was having trouble burying that torch.

She thought about all the fuss that had surrounded their marriage. You couldn't marry a man with his success secretly. It headlined all the newspapers and magazines. She became a household name. And then it had ended as abruptly as it had started. The fairytale drama had become a horror film.

After she left the days had turned into weeks, the months into years. The gulf expanded and grew until the memory began to fade. The pain turned into a nagging ache and then emptiness. But seeing him brought back all those nagging memories. The emptiness now an unbearable need. It felt like her heart was being crushed with a vise. The pain of his rejection steadily increasing. She still craved his touch. She wanted him with all the pent-up passion she had thought she'd buried for good.

. . .

Santo watched her go. He wanted to stop her, but he didn't. He hadn't expected her to show up for Nonna, but she had. He hadn't factored in all the pent-up desire, had he? She was beautiful, maybe even more so, than before. She looked fragile, skittish, jaded, and lost. Had he done that to her?

He knew he had. He remembered the way her lips trembled beneath his. The way she said his name. Hot streaks of need slammed through his body. He thought he'd bottled all the repressed desire inside. Yet, her unexpected appearance, brought it all back to the forefront of his mind.

He wasn't proud of the past. Of their failed relationship. He had been with many women, but he'd never given his heart, except to Maddie. Yes, he could admit it, she had gotten to him, still could, but was it love. He didn't think so. More an addiction. Something he couldn't get enough of no matter how hard he tried.

Time and distance should have curbed that addiction, but the craving was still there. He had messed up by kissing her, it only intensified the desire. At thirty-three he'd reached the top of his game. A pinnacle he'd worked so hard to acquire. He was successful, wealthy, had all that money could buy, but he was lonely. So lonely. And now his confidante, his support, and voice of reason had died, he had no one.

The villa felt empty, strangely haunting, and so big. He didn't even have a dog to keep him company. The staff came and went, but he barely saw them. Is this what he wanted? No wife, no children, no one to grow old with?

Maddie was mistaken about Vanessa's child,

but he'd not been given the chance to explain. She wouldn't listen nor believe him. She'd drawn all these conclusions, and he had let her. She'd believed with all her heart and soul that he'd betrayed their marriage vows. He hadn't. He'd been hurt by the accusations, so hurt in fact, that he'd let her go two years ago. There had been no phone calls, no texts, no explanations just hurt.

Unbearable hurt and misery.

His colleagues had stayed clear of him for months. His business deals became ruthless and un-forgiving. He'd worked nonstop and travelled many miles.

Santo had always been a tower of strength. Only one person had cracked his armor, Maddie Adams.

• • •

Maddie awoke to a loud pounding. At first her groggy brain couldn't detect what it was. Her eyes tried to adjust to the dark. The door.

Who on earth would be pounding on her room door, she looked at the bedside clock, at 5 o' clock in the morning?

She leaped out of bed, disoriented and scared. What was happening? An emergency? A fire?

Turning on the light she sniffed but didn't

smell anything. The pounding continued.

"Just a second," she mumbled, stumbling to the door.

Yanking it open, steely grey eyes, furiously glared at her. His athletic frame filled the opening. What was happening? She tried to surmise what he was doing.

"Santo?"

He barged into the room. "What did you do? How did you ever pull this off?" The ferocity of his voice boomed around the small confines of the space.

"What are you doing?" Maddie asked, puzzlement written across her face. "What are you talking about?"

"Nonna," he growled heatedly. "How did you convince her to do this? Blackmail," he quizzed, his eyes daring her to look away in denial.

And then he saw her, her curls wild and disorderly from sleep. Her lips puckered and moist. And her silky pajamas outlining the curves underneath. His blood boiled in his veins. Desire kickstarted in his gut and flowed to various other regions.

Instant desire filled his eyes. Maddie's heartbeat went into overdrive. His seduction skills were topnotch. Nothing lacking in that department. He'd always been a master at turning her on. Molten hot lava erupted in her. Her nipples pebbled. His eyes lit with fire. The always well groomed, collected, Santo Barrella, looked wild and unruly. Her erratic heart continued to pound against her chest. Yet, she still didn't know what had driven him to come pounding on the door. Why he looked like a storm cloud about to burst with torrential rains. Ferocious and furious.

"What are you ranting about, Santo? Why are you busting into my room at this ungodly hour spouting accusations?"

He gave her the onceover, the desire raging. The atmosphere sizzled with its intensity. He paced the room, disgust written upon his face. Her heart clenched with sorrow. "I talked to Nonna's solicitor this morning," he turned back and pinned her with his look, "she left you the villa!"

The desire in Maddie's veins instantly chilled, "What?" Maddie gasped. Shock filling her.

A sneer curved upon his lips. "Casa de Barrella has been in our family for over a hundred years. Whatever Ponzi scheme you've concocted it will never stick. Get dressed," he ordered, "we are getting this settled right now."

Maddie was confused and disoriented. Why would his grandmother do such a thing? She'd never accept it. The thought was absurd. Her mind buzzed with jumbled thoughts and scenarios. Her panic increased. This couldn't be happening. Surely, he'd misunderstood. Nonna wouldn't leave her the villa. It was sacred. A Barrella shrine. She put her hand upon her chest. Her racing heart pounding against her palm.

"This is crazy, Santo. I never told Nonna anything. I'm as shocked as you."

"Save the lies, Maddie!" His jaw flexed, trying to contain his frustration. "Get dressed!"

He was pacing relentlessly. His indomitable, arrogant eyes unreadable. She eyed him, waiting for him to leave the room, but he just stared daring her to disobey him.

"Once you leave I will get dressed," she demanded. Her heaving chest attracted his steady gaze. Her heart was ruthlessly crushing against her ribcage. Maddie cursed under her breath. Goosebumps were prickling against her over sensitized skin. Increased panic consumed her. She waited for him to depart inhaling deeply, even breaths to ward off the anxiety.

"I'll wait for you in the lobby. Five minutes!" He spun on his heel and left the room.

Maddie tried to unbutton her top with shaking fingers. She fumbled with the obstinate buttons. She was overwhelmed, not at Santo's fury, but from Nonna's decision. It made no sense. Nonna knew her as well as anyone. They'd grown so close during her stay in Italy. What possessed her to do it? Desperation? Nonna's last words to her were about forgiveness. Was this forced proximity? Guilt filled her conscience. She couldn't forgive him. He'd broken her heart, her will to go on.

She shook her head. Guessing would get her nowhere. She knew Santo, if she wasn't downstairs in the allotted time, he'd come looking for her making her heart pound even harder.

She threw her pajamas on the bed and dressed quickly. Brushing her hair and teeth she stuffed everything into her case and pulled it from the room. She had to be out this morning. Her flight was in the afternoon. This was a small hiccup with her departure plans. Once she was in flight all these emotions would dissipate. Then everything would be back to right. Getting back home and into her routine would bring back a semblance of order.

She found Santo pacing impatiently downstairs. Checking out at the front desk took only a few minutes. She waited for him to reach her side.

"Come on," he said, holding the door open for her and taking her suitcase.

The city was bustling with activity, but all she could sense was his red-hot electricity. The meticulously well-groomed Santo sported unshaved stubble on his square jaw making her handsome, billionaire husband, look almost human. Seeing his less than stellar appearance slightly flawed was a novelty. He was one of those men who woke up refreshed looking like a runway model. It always annoyed the heck out of her because she spent endless hours perfecting her appearance.

He opened the door to a shiny black sedan. Even with all his money and good looks, Santo had never been into flashy sports cars that drew attention. He had always preferred anonymity and solitude. Yet, the reporters always sought him out, posting his handsome good looks on the covers frequently.

Her stomach clenched when she thought of all the times she seen his handsome, brooding face paired with a beautiful socialite. The glossy cover photos of him illustrated the arrogant, gorgeous side of him. Even the boring business section became hot, hot, hot, with him sporting one of his glitzy designer suits. The stylists were proud to put him in one of their latest creations. Maddie had learned to avoid the articles because it led to more unbearable hurt.

She snapped her seatbelt, ordering the memories to disappear and fade. She pursed her lips together with annoyance. Nerves screamed up her neck and across her shoulders. Now all she had do was prevent herself from having a nervous break-down. All her yoga deep breathing exercises were coming in quite handy.

Santo climbed in. He slid into the driver's seat with catlike grace. Tall and broad, his exquisite body dominated the tight space. His jaw worked. His fingers gripped tightly onto the wheel. He brief-ly glanced at her. "I regret being angry," he said, "but the last few days have been hell for me."

"And that excuses it?" She looked down at her clasped hands and forced her stiff fingers to ease up on the death grip on the handle of her purse.

"No excuses," Santo countered, his predato-ry smile encompassing her. "The fact is I want this handled immediately so I can send you back home."

Heat burned her cheeks. His deep, husky accent skated along her already over-sensitized flesh. His desire to be rid of her so quickly was still a crushing blow. "Well, I'm sorry your grandmother dwarfed your plans. You can't buy your way out of every situation, Santo. Some things are air tight and require certain repercussions."

Her mocking tone made it clear he hadn't of-fended her. Was she heartless? Destroying his life, now his home.

The car lurched into the traffic. His concentration fully occupied for several minutes. When he spoke, his rough voice grated against her nerve endings. He looked at her intently. "Don't try to beat me at my own game, cara. You won't win," he focused on her mouth, hunger filled his charcoal grey eyes.

Her soft, indrawn breath captured his immediate attention. She blatantly stared at him. She didn't care that he knew how he still affected her. This would be the last time she'd get to embed his features into her memory bank. The last time she'd be able to touch that strong profile that had seduced her so many times. And before she realized what she was doing her hand reached out to clasp his jaw. Caress it.

He caught her hand in mid-air. "Don't!"

Chapter 3

Her heart plummeted.

He dropped her hand, and she placed it back in her lap. His rejection hurt. He was her vulnerability. Her weakness. But everyone must overcome weaknesses. Her included. She'd done a really good job, until now.

A double dose of rejection. It hurt like hell. Color rushed to her heated cheeks. What had she been thinking? Their relationship was tedious at best. He wanted her gone. Back out of his life and country. As soon as he straightened out this little hiccup, in the way, he'd send her packing.

There was no escaping herself. Running never stopped your heart from cravings it desired. She'd tried it.   The years had lessened it, but it didn't go away.

She wasn't much of a crier. She tried to avoid tears. They were a sign of vulnerability and weakness. They never solved anything. Generally, they made her feel worse.

This man, called husband, had plenty of scars, but he could be broken. Tamed. She'd seen the softer side of him before. He had let her into his head once. He'd spoken to her about his dreams, his desires, his future. But those days were over and had been for a long time. She must accept that and go on. Her mental stability counted on her success. Wanting to touch him was a continued curse. Her continued nemesis.

They came to a bank of office buildings. He pulled the car into a parking slot and turned off the ignition. Without a word he came around and opened her door. She refused his extended hand. Always the gentleman.

She followed his svelte form into the solicitor's office. His stoic expression gave no indication of his feelings. A young, chic girl looked up from her computer. No introduction was needed as soon as the receptionist saw Santo, she ushered them straight back.

The office was big, but cluttered. Stacks of files covered the desk and were piled along the wall on the floor. The lawyer raised his bespectacled eyes and smiled.

"Please be seated," the older, gray-haired man said, indicating two chairs.

Santo placed his hands upon the desk and gave the solicitor a demanding look. His formidable chest heaved with derision. His brow remained arched, and his eyes were piercing. "I've got her here," he stated flatly, "now tell us what's going on." His authoritative tone brooked no argument.

The lawyer smiled pleasantly. "You knew your grandmother, Santo, she was a head-strong woman. Much like yourself."

"She was also a savvy woman and didn't make rash decisions," Santo countered.

"Nor was this one," he continued. "She knew exactly what she wanted and was very clear about it. She was a force to be reckoned with, your grandmother."

"I don't need you to outline my grandmother's traits," Santo stated briskly. "I knew her quite well. Let's skip the small talk, shall we?"

"Fine, fine," he shuffled several papers upon his desk, while pushing the glasses upon his nose. "Here it is, right here."

He rifled through the sheaf of papers then shoved the papers toward Santo.

Santo scanned the documents intently and thoroughly before looking up. His petulant glance encompassed both of them.

"See," the solicitor said, "it's all neat and tidy."

Santo's brow furrowed in dismay. "How can we undo this?" His voice came across harsh.

"I can't," the lawyer apologized emphatically. Maddie tried to read the words, but Santo laid his arm across the print. "Why wasn't I ever informed of this?"

"Because, she knew what you would do." The old man eyed him confidently. He was firm and self-assured.

"Of course, she knew what I would do," he demanded. "The villa is my ancestral home. Maddie's not family."

"I'm afraid," the lawyer said quickly, "legally she is."

Maddie had enough. They were ignoring her blatantly insulting. She didn't like being talked over. Her heart was racing, her stomach was sick, and she was frantically trying to remain calm. She was disgusted with them and herself. Her heart took on an unsteady rhythmic beat.

"Would someone tell me what's going on? Quit acting like I'm not even in the room." Maddie glared at the two men forcefully.

They both looked at her, finally taking notice. "Santo's grandmother has left you the villa with one stipulation, you must produce an heir."

Maddie's heart nosedived. "And if I don't?" she asked curiously.

"Then the villa will be donated to the church," the lawyer stated emphatically.

"This is ludicrous," Santo paced across the room anger vibrating in his voice. His mouth quirked exasperation clearly reflected in his glance.

The color blanched from Maddie's face. "This means that Santo and I..." She couldn't continue.

She shivered with discomfort. The image of lying in his bed, his lips, his hands—she callously cut off the forbidden thoughts. Her eyes squeezed shut. The vision cleared. Her head hurt. She was being thrown into an impossible situation.

"And," the solicitor continued ominously, "this heir must be created within the next year."

She shook her head fiercely. "Oh, my gosh," Maddie's lungs tightened she was near hyperventilating. Her breathing became labored. "You're sure," she begged, "there are no loopholes?"

He threw his hands up as he pushed away from the desk. "Afraid not. It's simple. If you want the Casa de Barrella to stay in the Barrella family then produce an heir. Oh," he held up a finger, "and you must remain married and live together in the villa."

The old man outlined all the stipulations as if it was simple. When in fact it was anything but simple. The entire scenario was absolutely ridiculous. Maddie felt hysteria rising within her chest. The pressure was suffocating.

"What?" Her mouth twisted. Maddie felt faint from the sudden onset of dizziness that engulfed her. "Impossible. We can't. You see I can't stay with my husband."

The solicitor rose from his chair and came

around his desk. "I'll leave that for the two of you to work out," he smiled, as he ushered them out the door. "Please keep in touch, Santo, so I can make the necessary arrangements accordingly." With that he dismissed them. Maddie glanced at Santo. He wasn't happy.

Maddie was stunned, dazed. How had this happened? Nonna had exacted her authority from the grave. She knew they wouldn't come together willingly. So, she'd outsmarted her grandson. Giving him an ultimatum. Santo didn't like stipulations or ultimatums. In his business dealings he refused to submit to them.

Santo marched from the building, his shoulders stiff. His eyes flashed fiercely. "I'll get my legal team on this immediately. Something must be done."

Her steps faltered. Her head reeling with the dismal state of affairs. She watched Santo. A muscle pulsed in his jaw. His face a mask of unrest. She was vexed to think he wanted rid of her so much. His determination to undo his grandmother's wishes caused a twitch of regret and sorrow to fill her belly. Even though she knew it was the right thing to do. A small seed of hope nagged at her.

"Yes, Santo, fix this. I'm counting on you." He stopped in his tracks, and she nearly barreled

into his back. Turning he snarled at her, "How asi-
nine of you." He cast her a dark, menacing look. "I
should've never left you and Nonna alone.

I should've trusted my gut instincts. Trusting
you was a mistake. I let my guard down yet again.
Foolish..."

Straightening her spine with sheer pride,
Maddie stopped immediately. Heat prickled her
face. "I didn't destroy us the first time, and I won't
be blamed for this."

"You said you wanted me, didn't you? Well,
how convenient," he snarked, "the best of all
worlds. Me, a baby, and my home. What a come-
back."

The threat of unwanted tears clouded the
back of her eyes. She couldn't show that kind of
weakness right now. She smiled, remotely confident
Santo would find a way out of this. "Believe what
you will," she told him, "but I didn't influence your
grandmother in any way. This is one hundred percent her doing and her way of repairing our sham of
a marriage.

He snorted. "Sham being the key word. Get
in," he said, opening the door. "Call the airlines,
cancel your flight, until I get this thing worked out."
Hot sweat covered her body. She couldn't even feel
insulted that he was asserting full control. She nod-

ded.

He drove to the Barrella headquarters. She waited in the car making necessary phone calls. Cancelling her flight, rearranging schedules and responsibilities at home. It was hard to explain so she kept it brief.

She called Edward and told him she would be extending her stay. He wasn't happy, but grudgingly agreed. Guilt filled her. She'd made so many promises that she couldn't keep. This set of events were not within her control.

She was on edge. Her nerves stretched tight. Her throat felt scratchy and dry. At home she jogged several days a week to combat the daily stress. She hadn't done that for several days, and she could tell. The bad endorphins were taking over the good creating a dark moodiness.

Santo still hadn't exited the building, and she was beginning to get quite restless. Opening the door, she got out and stretched her stiff muscles. She paced around the vehicle. She tried to sort through the myriad of reasons causing her uneasiness. Yet, it came marching right back to one, Santo. His deep voice and foreign accent left her feeling deeply bothered. But his arrogance and deep-seated accusations made her anger spike quickly at his unfairness.

Then, she saw him striding toward her. Not good news she surmised. His dark, brooding look told the story. He halted before her. He speared her with his dazzling, intense grey eyes.

"Well," she jumped right in. "Did they come up with a solution?"

His stunning good looks a deterrent. She still selfishly craved Santo, but she wanted her freedom. A choice, not an arrangement.

"Yes," he stated calmly.

Whoosh. Her breath exited her lungs. Relief flooded through her bloodstream, bringing instant calm. "What did they say?"

"Welcome home, Mrs. Barrella," he replied sarcastically. "You're stuck with me."

Her mouth dropped open in shock. She tried to laugh, but it came out as a mousey squeak. "No." He looked at her. He didn't like it. Not one bit. He made a split-second decision. "You heard me, nothing we can do. Like it or not, this is our only choice."

She compressed her lips. "I won't do it. I can't," she whispered softly. "Wealth and power can't buy love, create children."

She clasped her middle. The thought of Santo's child in her womb formed a bittersweet craving. In all fairness it wasn't his fault she was still carrying a burning torch for him. She had invested so many hours trying to forget him but failed. Crystal clear clarity shined brightly. She wanted to keep this man close. She wanted to devote more time into their relationship. The thrill of capturing his tightly coiled energy frightened her. His resentment toward her wafted out in droves. Could she soften his heart ever again?

His dark brow shot up. He raked his hand through his hair, impertinence evident upon his face. "This wasn't my decision. But, I can't risk losing the villa. Like I said we have no choice."

Maddie was in a quandary. She didn't know what to do. She felt trapped. Helpless. Scared. Her skin blanched noticeably. His sheer charisma was domineering. Waves of nervousness shot along her spine.

"Get in," he said, impatience bouncing off him.

A retort nearly tripped off her tongue, she clamped her mouth shut to stop the rebellion. His arrogance was more intimidating than she cared to admit. Then to her utter surprise, he tipped up her chin and tucked a stray tendril behind her ear. A zap of sizzling electricity went firing down to her very core.

She stiffened, momentarily stunned by her

fiery response to a simple, harmless touch. The cool greyness of his eyes caught and held hers. She wanted to jerk away to regain her equilibrium but didn't. The blazing heat of her awareness stained her cheeks.

He drew his thumb across her lower lip. She bit down hard on the sensitized skin.

His lips quirked with amusement. He was laughing at her barely contained response. He reveled in the power he so easily wielded over her. She was hopelessly and completely aroused. And he knew it. His hand dropped, and he stepped away. Her body eased in relief. Desire a blessing, but a curse.

He opened the door, placing his hand on the back of her spine. A tiny sob escaped from between her lips. She heard his intake of breath. They were playing a dangerous game. Seduction had a powerful pull. She settled herself into the seat removing out of his touch. She released a strained laugh when she smacked her knee in her rush.

Once inside he started the engine of the powerful car and directed it back on the road toward home. The miles flew by in silence. His tall frame and wide shoulders filled up the car's interior. Making the space fill claustrophobic. Maddie tried to read his expressions, but he was stoic.

She wondered what he was thinking. Santo had never been big on sharing his feelings. It was black or white with no gray matter in between. While women's feelings were every color of the rainbow. And up and down, all around, and everywhere like a yo-yo. She surmised they truly had no choice but to brazen this out. The tension in the car was excruciating. Panic begin to set in again. She tried desperately to find a plausible excuse to get on the plane and fly home. Nothing came to mind. She couldn't think of one single concrete solution to their problem.   The cool leather of the seat moderated her over heated body temperature gaining her some semblance of control against her rioting emotions.

Maddie was still in shock from the day's events. Trying to wrap her mind around all that had been said. Nonna sure knew how to throw a ringer into their well thought out plans.

He parked the car. She sat locked in her seatbelt. She battled with the elemental urge to ease closer to him, and let the overwhelming longing consume them. She knew it was foolish thoughts. She shifted in her seat unlatching the clip on the side. The sumptuous black leather interior felt cramped. He unlatched his seatbelt and leaned across the middle console. His face mere inches from hers. His gaze was intent. Raising his hand his knuckles lightly brushed her cheek.

"Why are you so nervous, caro? Is the thought of making a baby with me so repulsive, hmm?"

"It's not that," she blurted out looking around for a plausible excuse to bail out and scramble from the car.

"Then relax," he smiled suddenly. "It's not like I'm going to carry you in the house, throw you on the bed, and ravage you. I may be a neanderthal, but I have more class than that."

"Stop," she reproached valiantly. The visceral image of him using caveman tactics sent disturbing, kinky images clinking through her mind.

His staggeringly intense grey eyes studied her. Multiple sensory sensations skated along her spine, making her lungs feel devoid of oxygen.

"I promise you, Maddie, I expect nothing from you. If a child is created out of this we will do so willingly together," he said, cryptically.

How easily he could weave his sensual spell around her. Prickling sensations ripped over her skin. She knew he meant it. Succumbing to his charms was almost second nature. Hopefully she had enough willpower to resist.

He leaned back into his seat. She couldn't look straight into his eyes for fear of him seeing into her thread bare soul. And despite her noble attempt at defense she was weak, weak, weak. There was evidence of her tender heart exponentially being broken again. He had one distinct advantage. He'd already captured her war-torn heart before.

Santo looked at her before stepping from the car, and Maddie felt an unspoken understanding filter between them, instinctively she shivered. She hoped he found a solution and quick.

He unloaded the luggage and carried it through the door. She hadn't packed for an extended stay. She'd need to shop for some much-needed essentials until they could sort this thing out. Maddie exhaled deeply trying to keep it together. Her mind was jumbled with the unknown.

Once inside Santo clasped her elbow and marched her to his office off the entryway. The room was basked in sunlight, and she blinked to adjust her eyes. Leading her to a chair, he moved behind his desk. The large piece of wooden furniture presented a barrier between them. As if one didn't already exist.

Santo drummed his fingers upon the surface of the desk. She watched mesmerized nearly in a trance. The rhythm pounded in her head. As his fingers drummed his brow furrowed deeply. There was something going on in that analytical mind of his. She could feel it. She clutched her forehead to ease the nagging headache. The day had been grueling. She waited for him to speak. The silence became

deafening. Her chest was filled with a void hollow-
ness. What were they going to do? She felt trapped.
Numb. Maddie felt emptiness. Finally, he spoke.

"I don't know what Nonna was thinking,"
he threw out briskly, "but it's irrelevant now." He
combed his fingers through his hair, the glint in his
eyes molten steel. "We've been thrown into this
partnership by circumstance. We'll take it to the
finish line."

Maddie's heart plummeted. There he went
again. Turning this into a business deal. No feeling,
no compassion, and certainly no love. Her horizon
looked so bleak. After all the loss, the pain, misery,
torment, and then healing, she was right back at the
beginning. His glacial grey eyes were the same eyes
that haunted her waking hours and her dreams. Now
he sat right back in front of her tossing out com-
mands. She wasn't his employee, a rival, she was
his wife and would be treated as such. She almost
laughed, feeling faintly hysterical.

"Listen, Santo, I understand the dilemma
we're in," she clenched her fists open and shut. Her
nails biting into the tender flesh. He watched her
intently. She felt sick to the stomach. "Believe me,
I'm as shocked as you, but I'm not one of your well
thought out business plans. I have a heart, I have
feelings, and I have the right to defend myself."

He lifted a hand, anger prevalent in his voice. "Rights?" he laughed. "You waltz back into my life and cause nothing but useless havoc. You lost that privilege when you influenced Nonna with this incredulous notion to throw us together," Santo voice sounded rough, even to her.

He seemed hellbent on blaming her for this ridiculous situation. She was tired of his accusations. He epitomized the all powerful alpha male business tycoon. His forcefulness was actually a bit of a turn on. She wasn't able to repress a shiver of acute awareness that raced up her spine. The intensity that surrounded him oozed of danger. He was a perfect specimen of male masculinity. Darkly gorgeous.

But he always handled himself with the utmost respect. Never crossing the line. She admired it, his ability to remain in control. She on the other hand, was spontaneous, blunt, and to the point.

The threat of tears prickled at the back of her eyes. She refused to cry, and she wasn't about to give him the benefit of watching her do it now. She cleared her voice, "Stop it, Santo. Quit being a jerk. You and I both know that Nonna implemented this long before I returned. I haven't spoken to her, out of respect to you, until I came here."

She glared at his hard features. She'd known he worked hard, but she hadn't known him to ever look so stressed. His pale, drawn cheek bones looked more pronounced. His dark hair glistened under the artificial light while his jaw clenched with determination.

"Respect," he drew out the word with deliberate ease. "Is that what you call your feelings for me, respect?" He laid his forearms across the desk and leaned toward her, "I believe, amore mio, we lost that a long time ago."

His heavily accented words chilled her to the bone. She shivered. Goosebumps pinpricked upon her arms.

His brow rose questionably. "Are you cold?"

"No," she stated adamantly, "and don't whisper Italian endearments to me." The intense memories of those same words whispered into her ear, amongst satin sheets, crashed into her mind. Her memory bank became clouded with the ecstasy they had shared. Torturous memories, forgotten memories she'd catalogued in her mind, raced to the forefront. His gliding hands touching every erogenous zone on her body. The kissing, flirting, foreplay, and the culmination of all their pent-up desires. Tears swam in her eyes.

The grey-steeliness of his pupils softened, and redness shaded his cheek. She knew the same memory had crossed his mind.

"Maddie, although things fell apart in our marriage, the sex was good." His broad shoulders shifted.

What did she say to that? The charismatic reality was the sex had been more than good, it'd been great, mind-blowing, and heart-stopping.

"I won't lie, Santo, if our marriage had been based upon the bedroom alone, it deserved an A+. That's why," she said, sadly, "I don't understand why you sought comfort somewhere else?"

"Accidenti!" He leaned back and clasped his fingers together. "Our fate has been sealed," he tossed out without preamble. "Here's what I'll do," he commanded. "I'll give you Casa de Barrella," he paused for effect, "you give me an heir."

Chapter 4

She didn't think it could happen, but a very, very bad day had just gotten worse.

Maddie's body felt war-torn and beaten. The searing pain emanated like white-hot streaks zipping around her heart. She wanted him, she wanted his child, but not born from obligation.

"No, I don't want Casa de Barrella, Santo. I don't want any of this." She rubbed her aching brow. "Please, we have too much bad blood, too much history to ever mend. I just want to go home."

His eyes were callous. "No," he stated simply.

"I'm sorry about all of this. I'm sorry I came here. Listen," she briefly closed her eyes, "I don't want you to lose your ancestral home. You'll figure something out. You always do," she assured him. "It's best I leave here and never look back. A baby is out of the question."

"You had my loyalty," he said quietly. "Once."

She opened her eyes wide. "Oh, that's classic. Loyalty. How could you? You were loyal to only one person. You," she spat.

"You left me, Maddie. Without a word, without a note. Just left." His lips clipped together and the hard set of his jaw stiffened. "I thought you cared. I thought..." He stopped and looked away.

"Never mind what I thought. I need an heir. I'm not getting any younger. Who better than my wife to give me a child?"

His eyes glinted with hardness, merciless, and determined. She suddenly remembered all their closeness, sharing laughs, sharing impromptu meals, jet-setting around the world on his private jet. It had all seemed so real but had all been a fantasy. A foolish fantasy on her part.

"Why did you marry me, Santo?" She asked, bewildered. "You'd already seduced me. You knew you were my first. Why?"

"I don't know," he said simply. "I felt obligated." The tick in his jaw intensified, capturing her undivided attention. "I couldn't treat you like a one-night stand."

"So, you slept with me, married me, then betrayed my trust?" She raised her tear-stained eyes. "I'd rather been a one-night stand. Guilt-free and painless with no obligations."

"A piece of paper didn't stop you. You ran anyway," he said with a low voice.

"I couldn't stay," she replied softly. "I couldn't. What we had was a lie, still is. Let me go, divorce me. Get back your freedom."

"Freedom's not what I want," his tone softened. "It's you in my bed, and a baby in my arms."

His eyes narrowed into slits. His gaze roamed over her lips, her neck, then lowering to her pert breasts.

The intensity of his look scorched her skin. Her nipples pebbled, her breath held.

Desire stained his taut cheeks. The memory of their shared passion crashed upon her. She tried to look away but couldn't. He held her under his spell.   Mesmerized, tortured by the searing, hot, sensual details of his touch. Lord help her, but she had spent so many lonely nights dreaming about him. How he'd made love to her, brought her to such pleasure. Some things you could not forget. She closed her eyes, but his image remained. Intense longing lanced through her. No, she couldn't do this. She just couldn't.

He was the ultimate playboy. So irresistible, untamable. Yet, so many women had tried to capture him and couldn't. She'd gotten him to the alter, but at what price.

The ultimate price. The ultimate sacrifice. Her broken heart.

A twinge of uneasiness flowed through her. "And...if I agree. Then what? I bear a child into a loveless marriage. It will be thrown into a home with two parents who, although married, walk on eggshells every time they get near each other. What kind of life is that for a child?" Her eyes searched his face, pleaded with him to understand.

"I know the circumstances aren't the best." He rose from the chair and walked over and gazed out the window. "We can try. We can surely be civil to one another for the sake of our child."

"What then?" she asked when he turned back around. "The school term with me. The holidays with you. Shuffled back and forth like baggage. A constant game of tug-of-war. "It's not fair," she caught a sob deep within. "I wouldn't be able to live with myself. Could you?"

The greyness of his eyes deepened, darkened like blustery storm clouds. "It wouldn't be like that. Our child would not be shuffled back and forth. We would remain together," he demanded.

"Here," he waved his hand, "in the villa, in Florence."

"What about my life, my career?" She demanded, torn with regret. "My home and family?"

"And Edward?" His lips twisted. "The pathetic man follows you everywhere."

She gasped in outrage. "You're the one whose pathetic. Spying on my every move without my knowledge. Edward's only a friend, nothing more."

"Is that what you call it?" A twinge of jealousy crept into his voice. "Goodnight kisses, holding hands and late-night dinners, isn't that friends with benefits?"

"How dare you?" she wrapped her arms across her chest. "Don't drag my friendship with Edward through the gutter. At least he was there for me because you weren't."

He arched one dark eyebrow. "Then you don't deny it? He's your lover?"

"No," she reiterated. "Anyway, it's none of your damn business."

"Excuse me," he said softly, dangerously. "You are definitely my business."

His words fell upon her leaving no doubt he meant it.

He came around the desk and stood in front of her. Maddie scooted back in the chair to gain some distance, but he moved closer. He pinned her knee between his legs. Heat tore through her, causing tremors. He felt it.

He placed his hands upon the arms of the chair and leaned in until his eyes collided with hers. "You're mine Maddie," his voice rasped softly. "No matter how many men you allow into your life they will never claim you the way I have."

He slowly dipped his head, and his lips caught hers. A moan escaped her lips before she could stop it. His mouth was heavenly, firm, yet gentle, but demanding a response, which she so willingly gave. The kiss only lasted a few seconds, but it seemed like an eternity. He stepped back releasing her. Her heart pounded erratically. Her eyes felt huge upon her face. Just one kiss, and she was his. At that moment she would have promised him anything.

"And that is why you will be staying," he said. "The magic is still there. Just one touch, Maddie, and I need so much more. My body still burns for you, and yours for mine. You know the only way to satisfy this craving is for you to come to my bed." She shook her head, but the denial refused to escape her lips. Why try? It would be pointless to deny it.

"Tomorrow I will be gone for a couple days." He raked his hands through his hair. "I must catch up on some unfinished business. When I return we will finish this? I demand we reach a truce outside, and inside, the bedroom."

She met his unwavering look. No answer was needed.

Then he turned and left the room.

• • •

Maddie awoke to the smell of fresh coffee. Santo must have informed the help she was here before he left. She had heard him moving about before daylight, then the whirring of helicopter blades before it took off.

She hadn't slept much. Her brain had been racing. She tried without success to force sleep several times. Her thoughts had been to jumbled. Daylight was streaking the sky when she had finally dozed off. Now she felt like the morning after hang-over.

Only one week in Italy, and she'd felt like she'd been drug through hell and back. An emotional roller coaster ride. How could her feelings for one man put so much strain into her life?

Her eyelids felt heavy and swollen as she sat down at the table laid out for breakfast on the ter-race. The bright morning sunlight caused her to squint against its gleam.

"What can I bring you, Signora Barrella? Per-haps coffee and juice?"

The housekeeper waited for her response. She hadn't been addressed as Santo's wife for so long. She had forgotten what it sounded like.

"Yes, coffee, black, strong," she said with a smile.

"My name's Isabella, signora. Perhaps you would like some eggs, fruit?"

She waited for Maddie's direction.

"Croissants and fruit would be fine, Isabella.

Thank you."

"Yes, signora, right away."

As Isabella hurried away Maddie wondered where Santo had gone off to. Which city? How far? He hadn't told her much. What the heck would she do for a couple days? At home she was used to a busy schedule.

Her phone dinged. She frowned. Who would be texting her? The message was simple.

"Good morning, amore. I hope you slept well?"

She smiled against her better judgment. "Good, thank you." She typed back. He didn't need to know that his handsome face haunted her all night making sleep elusive.

"Make yourself comfortable while I'm gone," he dinged back. "I'll try to wrap this up as quick as I can. Missing you already."

She looked at his words. Butterflies danced in her belly. He missed her. She liked the sound of that. She couldn't believe it. Where had that come from? Shock tightened her insides.

"I'll try," she quickly replied, and left it at that. She waited for him to say something else, but he didn't. Disappointment filled her.

Isabella returned with her coffee and food. She looked out across the beautiful scenery and sipped her hot coffee. The countryside was so se-

rene, so lovely. She could get used to this in a hurry.
But she knew it wasn't easy. Trust and forgiveness
were hard to regain. Santo was pushing her too fast.
Wanting things, she wasn't ready to give. A baby
was a huge commitment. A life changing decision.
Was she ready for that? Giving him a part of herself
that would be forever. A child.

She clutched her tummy. Images of his child
growing there forming in her mind. So precious,
so helpless. She knew that she would make a good
mother. Her mother was a great example of moth-
erhood and what it should be. Her parents had been
married for forty-five years, and they made it look so
easy.

She'd grown up in suburbia New York. Her
mom a high school music teacher, her dad a profes-
sor. Both retired now. She had one brother, one
sister, both older, married with kids. She was the
only one without a family. Her mom often lectured
her on being married to a man and not living with
him. They never could understand their weird arrangement.

Her family had loved Santo, so they hadn't understood what had happened. Her mom had wanted
to hit him over the head with a broom when Maddie
had endured so much hurt from his betrayal.

Her mom still didn't believe it. She'd always
told her that a man with Santo's integrity would nev-

er do that to her. She had been so wrong. He had.

But, here she was in Italy, pining over him. A man who still turned her inside out with just one look.

A man she craved foolishly.

A man who could pull her right back into his web of seduction.

Wait until she called her mom and told her Santo wanted a child. Knowing her parent's, they would encourage her to think it over, but if she was going to stay married to the man it wouldn't be a bad idea.

But it was a bad idea, right?

She rose from the chair and thanked Isabella again for breakfast. She informed her she was taking a walk in the fresh air. It smelled of jasmine. As she walked along the road, birds whistling, the warmth of the sun upon her shoulders, she wished things weren't so complicated.

Her whirlwind romance with Santo had been exciting yet excruciating. He had lost his parents in a horrific car crash when only ten. His grandmother had raised him, doting on her only grandson. Santo had been an only child, so he had been so alone. His heart had been guarded, protected. Then they had met and fell instantly into lust. That's what she liked to call it these days because love didn't seem to apply.

Then that horrible night. They'd been at a charity ball Santo supported. Vanessa had been drinking heavily, making overt advances on Santo.

Jealousy had dug at her insides. Reared its ugly head. Growing ugly as the clock continued to tick. She refused to cause a scene amongst the ritzy, glittering crowd.

Maddie felt powerless to stop the interaction between the ex-lovers. Vanessa hands explored his chest, his broad shoulders, causing Maddie to flee the room in tears. Her heart had been torn to shreds. The hurt unbearable.

She'd thought he would come searching for her, but he hadn't. As the crowd dispersed she had gone looking for him. And she found him, locked in an embrace on the balcony, with his lips locked with Vanessa's.

Then the news, Vanessa's son, belonged to Santo.

Maddie had run, she had flown home, never to look back.

She looked around at the tranquil Italian countryside. It was an illusion. Instead of finding happiness, she found misery. The upside was Nonna had been so good to her. She'd treated her like the daughter she'd never had. They had spent so many wonderful hours together. A tear slid down her cheek, she missed the dear old lady and her wisdom. Maddie had walked nearly a mile before she turned and started her trek back. Walking, or jogging, usually was a natural stress reliever, but this morning didn't seem to help. She inhaled deeply. The fresh, country air helped ease her tension.

Her phone rang. She glanced at the screen and saw Santo's name. He'd shared his contact information the first day she had come back.

Sliding the bar, she answered. "Hello."

She clutched the phone tightly to her ear.

"Signora Barrella," he gushed politely. "How was breakfast?"

"Fine."

"What are you doing now?" He continued pleasantly.

"Why?" she asked automatically.

He laughed. "Did you wake up on the wrong side of the bed this morning, amore? I know what would fix that."

"Huh, no. As a matter of fact, I slept like a baby," she lied smoothly.

His deep, sexy laugh floated across the line. "Good," he responded, "but you still didn't answer my question."

"What question?" she pretended ignorance.

"Don't play coy with me, signora."

"Fine," she answered. "I'm taking a walk. Satisfied?"

"Yes," he stated flatly.

"How about you?" She countered. "Where are you? I thought you had meetings?"

"I do," he said, "I'm in between appointments. In London," he added.

"Oh," was all she managed to say.

"Listen, I need to go, but I'll see you soon, amore mio."

Then there was silence. He'd hung up. Maddie stared at the screen for several seconds before placing the phone back in her pocket. She didn't understand him at all. It was like the years of absence had slipped away. She was back on his playing field, and the odds were in his favor. You could never beat a man, on his own turf, at his own game. Impossible.

Maddie passed the day swimming, reading, and exploring the villa refamiliarizing herself with its splendid glory.

She ate a light lunch but skipped the evening meal. Isabella and her husband had a small cottage down the road. They informed her that they came daily and would be back in the morning.

Maddie awoke with a start. Disoriented and

groggy her eyes tried to focus in the dark. Something wasn't right. Where was she?

Then it all came crashing back. In the villa, under Santo's roof. Her legs were tangled in the sheets. She kicked them aside. Then she felt his presence before he spoke.

"You were snoring, tesoro."

Maddie sat straight up in the bed. Shocked. Santo was in her bedroom.

"What are you doing?" Maddie could barely see his outline sitting in the chair. Her eyes were having trouble focusing. "I don't snore," she retaliated.

"It was very appealing, amore, more like a purr."

She fumbled at the bedside until she found the lamp. Twisting the switch, soft light illuminated the room, casting away the shadows.
Santo was still fully dressed. His designer suit accentuating his superb form.

Maddie felt so inadequate with her wildly mussed hair, sleep in her eyes, and dry mouth. The ashen taste was bitter upon her tongue. She swallowed, rolling her dry tongue moistening it with saliva.

It was unfair that he looked so calm and put together. Even at this time of night. She squinted, focusing on the clock, at 2 o' clock in the morning.

"How long have you been sitting there, watching me," Maddie demanded.

"Not long," Santo rose from the chair and moved to the edge of the bed. Cornering her. His hand dropped upon her knee. The piercing depths of his eyes landed upon her face. Her skin burned from his touch.

Maddie quickly scooted over, avoiding his touch.

"Scared, Maddie?" He gave her that domineering, Santo look, that no one else could perfect.

"Should I be?" she shot back nervously.

"Yes," he said, while clamping her bare ankle beneath her pajama pants. His touch was electrifying. He gently massaged the area beneath his palm. Maddie wanted to pull away but felt helpless to end the contact.

His touch scorched her skin. His hand slid up her calf muscle causing it to contract with awareness. She sucked in large amounts of oxygen filling her distressed lungs.

"Your skin is so silky soft, tesoro," he whispered. "Just like I remember." The faint smell of his cologne wafted around her. Intoxicating her.

She needed to put a stop to this madness. But suddenly fierce need overtook her sanity. His touch was setting her on fire. She remembered the smell of him, the pleasure of his kiss. His touch had set her on fire so many times. He had a sensual power over her that she didn't want to resist.

His slumbering grey eyes encompassed her mass of wild curls. The gold flecks in her hazel eyes seemed to be more prominent from suppressed desire.

The days growth of stubble shadowed his cheek. She remembered the prickly, raspy scratch of his unshaved whiskers. A hunger so strong swept over her entire being. The past and present suddenly didn't matter. Only this man, her husband, mattered and how he made her feel. Hopelessly, needlessly burning up for this man's touch. Only Santo had this power over her. One touch from him, one kiss from his lips, and she was lost.

He removed his hand but reconnected, sliding them onto her thighs, onto her hips, until his hands spanned her slender waist. Santo craved her. While he was away he'd thought of nothing else. He wanted to push her onto the mattress put his hands into her hair and press his lips against hers until she whimpered his name.

Her breath hissed from within her lips. His hands seared her burning skin. She ached for the promise he was withholding. How could this be happening? She was like putty in his hands. Hadn't her Italian husband always had this power over her? She couldn't resist. She wanted him badly. Her heart pounded, her body flooded with uncontrollable wants and needs.

He was the king of sexual titillation. A master at seductive techniques. No woman could defy the mastery of his hands.

His body covered hers. Her breath held. The sensual slide of his body on top of her sent scorching hot tremors throughout her body. This was madness. Utter madness. She couldn't allow this torture to continue. She didn't want this, but yet, she did.

Then, his mouth found hers. His tongue gained entry into the moist cavern between her lips. She tasted the sweetness of wine, the sweetness of his lips. Whatever sanity she had been maintaining was quickly disappearing. She was tired of fighting this hold he had upon her. The seconds ticked by slowly. Agonizing seconds of pure torture. They could barely carry on a civilized conversation with each other, but in bed they were attuned to each other's every need. Like synchronized swimming routines they were perfectly choreographed.

Their clothes were a barrier. She tugged at the lapel of his coat. He struggled impatiently to remove the obstruction, tossing it to the floor.   Her hands spread the breadth of his shoulders, touching, feeling the tenseness of his muscles. She loosened his tie and tossed it aside.

His mouth continued to ravage her lips. Nipping, biting, sucking their lushness between his. He rolled to her side. His hands devoured her willing flesh. He travelled the path beneath her silky top and found the exposed mound of her supple breast.

He massaged its pert roundness. Her nipple hardened with delight. The moan of ecstasy came from her. His delighted chuckle sent shivers along her spine.

He knew she was under submission to his touch. He was in complete control. She could not deny him. He found her aching nipple and drew it into his mouth. He suckled the first one, and then the other. Her fingers tangled wildly in his hair. Tugging at the silky strands.

"Maddie," he groaned huskily. Her name sounded so erotic coming from him. Like a plea to satisfy his every desire.

She felt his stiff arousal imbedded against her hip. The years of abstinence flew from existence. It was like they'd never parted, never quit.

Her subconsciousness implored her to take control.
To stop this.

Pull away.

But his seductive power won. She ignored the threat. She allowed the powerful tide of desire to consume her. Blind her to the danger of compliance and the control it would give.

The sheen of arousal glimmered on her body. His tongue kept a constant barrage of lustful desire skimming across her chest.

Her golden curls tossed from side to side under the assault. She moaned with pleasure. The apex between her legs quivered with need. She arched her hips, bucking beneath his touch.

He lifted his head. His cool grey eyes darkened with lust. His lips compressed with barely contained control.

"Say you want me, amore. Tell me how you feel. What you want." He prompted as his lips grazed her cheek, then the corner of her mouth.

Maddie swallowed. Somehow, she had parted the buttons of his shirt. His olive chest rippled beneath her fingertips. She squeezed his aureole between her thumb and forefinger. She felt impowered from the breath that hissed from between his compressed lips. His pupils dilated from arousal.

"Oh, I want you," she said, the words sounded like a satisfied purr coming from her lips. "Your sexual prowess was never the problem, Santo."

He groaned his pleasure. He found the heat at the center of her core. She was wet, she was ready, she was completely on fire.

He whispered sweet nothings as his hand made a path to the waist of her pajamas. He made a path of sweet discovery until his fingers invaded her sensitive center.

"So hot, tesoro. So ready for me."

She swallowed quickly. As his fingers made contact with her bud the sparks begin to flow. Her fingers gripped his shoulders. She squirmed beneath him. She couldn't hardly breathe. Santo certainly hadn't lost his touch. If anything, it seemed more intense than ever before.

He plied at her bringing her to the cusp of surrender. The voice of reason pounded at her to call a halt. To stop this invasion upon her senses. But she was powerless to move.

He had commandeered her common sense, her reason, her ability to say no. Maddie had always prided herself on her tenacity and control. But just one touch from this man and everything she knew, or could think, vanished.

Poof! Nothing but stimulated nerve endings, and the culmination of desire, gained control. Layer upon on layer of pleasure begin to build, about to reach its crescendo, sending her over the edge.

"That's it baby," he softly whispered in her ear, "stay with me. So forthcoming, so unbearably sweet. You may have physically left me, Maddie, but your body never has." He laughed proudly.
His mocking words stilled her. She was on the brink of orgasm, but his self-assured cockiness broke the magic evil spell.

She placed her hand upon his wrist, halting the continued precision. It took everything she had to withstand his glorious seduction. But she must. Heart pounding, she sat up in the bed, bringing her knees beneath her chin.

He looked at her, confusion written upon his face.

"This isn't the answer," she hissed, "seducing me because you can."

He raised his eyebrows. Encompassing her sex-induced, tousled appearance. "I never heard you complaining or asking me to stop."

"You caught me off guard. You woke me from a sound sleep."

"You want me," his cloudy, grey eyes took in the rise and fall of her fully outlined breasts. "Why deny your own pleasure?"

"My body wants you, but my mind says no."
She crossed her arms to shield her swollen breasts.
"Our pleasure, Santo, is only a small piece of this

puzzle. There are so many hurdles to climb."

"A solid relationship starts with mind-blowing sex," he said unabashedly.

"You're wrong," Maddie said, pulling her knees up even tighter. "A solid relationship starts with love, trust, and commitment, which we don't have any of those."

"It's been a wild ride." Santo's sexy countenance appeared unruffled. "Just like old times."

She stood needing to leave the shared bed and putting distance between them. He linked his fingers behind his head and leaned against the headboard.

She frowned. "It's nothing like old times. I'm not that star-struck innocent girl from three years ago. I learned the hard way not to trust pretty words and an incredible body."

She paced the confines of the space, tempted to break her resolve and finish where they had left off. His dark, olive skin contrasted against the whiteness of the sheets did something crazy to her equilibrium.

Santo was the kind of man that dominated a room, dominated the bedroom. Her heart beat a rapid staccato against her chest.

She stopped and eyed him fiercely. "I came here to see your grandmother. I didn't know it was for the last time." She clasped the cuffs of her pajamas and tugged. "These added complications weren't expected."

Santo noted her nervousness. She was restless and cagey. Unfulfilled satisfaction did that to a person. He knew because he felt the same way. "Expected, or not," he said, uncurling his tall frame from the bed, "they need to be dealt with. I don't intend to let you leave again without bedding you. Our mutual attraction still exists, amore. You must admit that."

She'd be foolish to disagree. The more she refuted his words, the more apt he was to seal the deal. "You're right," she admitted. "But sexual desire doesn't need to be appeased."

"Doesn't it? In our case it does." He looked at her almost apologetically. "No matter the number of cold showers, this fire in my blood has only one possible solution." He smiled, confidently. "You."

He was determined to have her, tame her wild spirit.

Her hazel eyes defied him. They danced with his making him realize that, in fact, she was not the young, vulnerable girl she had once been. He might claim her body, but he was going to have to work hard to claim her heart.

The past demanded that he must prove him-

self all over again. She would accept nothing less.
Although she had left him without so much as a note,
he'd remained devoted to her memory. Sure, he
tried to take out his frustrations with other wom-
en, have sex with them, but he couldn't. Maddie's
memory clouded his mind causing him to pull away.
Three years of faithfulness was hard on a man. Especially a virile, healthy, man.

But now that she was back, she was worth it.

The fire was voracious.

"Why appease this wild desire, only to tear it
back apart?" she said. "I don't think I can do it all
over again, Santo. I need someone safe, comfortable, dependable. Someone I can count on and that
isn't you."

"Who? Edward? Mr. Dependability." He
couldn't stop the infliction of jealousy that entered
his voice.

She was surprised at the possessiveness that
crept into his voice. Was he jealous? Did that mean
there was some feeling in that cold, hard muscle
called a heart?

"That's none of your business. If I choose Edward, once we're divorced, there's nothing you can
do about it." Her eyes defied him once again.

He stepped toward her. His exposed muscles coiled and tight. "There's that forbidden word
again, divorce. I'm not a generous man, in some

instances, and on this I'm firm."

He cupped her cheek with the palm of his hand. Her blood stirred immediately. So quickly, so easily, he turned her on. Actually, she never turned off.

"You're mine, tesoro." His thumb brushed across her lips. "And no man will take what is mine."

Maddie bit her lip. How could he be so calm, and yet, exerting this control over her body, her response. In that moment she wanted him but hated him. She felt so helpless beneath his hands. A powerful drug that took away her reason, her sanity.

He went to claim her lips again, but she turned away. She couldn't allow him to have this power over her. She had to think clear and rational. Exhibiting the willpower to resist this man for good.

His eyes projected his irritation. But he stepped away respecting her wishes.

"Good night, my sweet, defiant Maddie. This is far from finished."

And he turned and walked from the room, leaving her aching for something she knew she couldn't have.

Chapter 5

Numerous nights of very little sleep were starting to take its toll on Maddie's appearance. Dark circles haunted her eyes and paleness shadowed her cheeks. She looked gaunt. Unhealthy.

This battle of the wills was putting a massive strain upon her. It was making her an emotional train wreck.

She found Santo sitting on the terrace, coffee in his hand, looking cool, collected, and so put together.
His hair glistened from his morning shower, his early morning stubble completely gone.

The morning sunshine cast its heated rays upon her shoulders. She lifted her face toward its light absorbing its welcome heat.

"Please, help yourself," Santo said, indicating the table spread full of breakfast choices.

She took the seat across from him and sat down. It had already been an unsettling morning. Sleep depravation did weird things to the body. She was irritable and didn't care if he knew it or not. Denying him last night, denying herself, had been extremely difficult. Seeing him looking so fine when she looked like hell made her even more grumpy.

"Coffee," he inquired. His lean, strong face was disconcerting.

She nodded her head. Pursing her lips together to keep from snapping childishly. Picking up a
croissant she tore off a small piece and put it in her
mouth chewing the soft, fluffy bread. Then she followed the bite with a sip of coffee.

"You look tired," he noted, looking concerned
by her appearance. "Aren't you sleeping?"

"You know the obvious answer to that," she
grimaced.

A smile graced his lips. "You must take care
of yourself. Eat healthy, exercise, and get plenty of
rest."

She stiffened her spine and rolled back her
shoulders and then glared at him. His rigid high
cheekbones tensed, and he ground his perfectly even
white teeth with consternation. She only glared
more.

He nearly rolled his eyes at her outrageously
childish pout. He raked his glossy dark hair back
from his brow in an impatient gesture.

"Thanks for the advice," she clipped, moodily.
"I can take care of myself."

He cradled his cup between his hands. His
eyes met and held hers. He was so outrageously
handsome. He leaned forward brooding reflections
piercing the vibrant pools of his gaze.   "You need to
be in top-notch condition to have our child."

She tossed him an exasperated look. "Really? You're worried about if I'm healthy enough to produce a child. How clinical of you."

He had the audacity to thrown back his head and laugh heartily. "You are way too serious, amore."

She was trying very hard to take offense, but it was good to see him laugh. The last few days had put such a dark shadow upon him. But, she wasn't about to tell him. "I don't find it funny. Having a baby is a very serious and big decision. One I refuse to take lightly."

"Nor do I." He leaned across the table to refill his coffee.

The talk of a baby sent her maternal instincts nosediving. Maddie looked across at the scenery strategically changing the subject. "It's a beautiful morning. What are you doing today?"

He shrugged. "I have a few calls to make, then I thought I'd spend the day with you."

She looked back at him surprised. "Really? Why?"

She didn't want to spend the day with him. She was already on an emotional rollercoaster with him in the same vicinity. An entire day of his company would be unbearable. She wouldn't be able to handle it.

Santo rarely took a day off work. Especially since he'd been absent the last few days. She didn't think he'd even allow personal days to his employees. He was a hard task master. Giving as good as he got.

"What would you like to do," he continued, ignoring her startled expression, "go shopping? Sightseeing? Beach? Or straight to bed?"

Her heart somersaulted within her chest. He was incorrigible. He relentlessly tossed in the bedroom jibes. Their attraction was an ever-constant temptation. And he used it.

She gave him a frown. Choosing to ignore his last question. "I do need to pick up some things. So, shopping would be great."

Shopping would be safe. Large crowds with not much of an opportunity to be alone. Being alone with Santo rattled her senses, making her want to rush to his bed.

"Fine," he said. "Shopping it is. Get your things, and I'll meet you at the car."

He came around and pulled out her chair, brushing her shoulder. She shivered from his touch. The thin straps of her blue dress left the skin exposed giving him easy access. The pad of his thumb ran one last path across the sensitive area before he stepped back.

She quickly and clumsily exited the chair and headed to her room. Once inside she took a deep breath regaining her composure. How could she spend an entire day with him without becoming a frazzled set of nerves?

The memories of the early morning came rushing back to cause her even more misery. Snatching her purse, she left the room.

She found him waiting near the black sedan. A cherry red sportscar was parked beside it. She eyed the automobile before casting him a curious look. "When did you buy this?"

He had disposed of his jacket and was wearing a cool, gray shirt that accentuated the steeliness of his eyes. The silver-grey color was the exact lustrous shade of a polished shard of metal. Maddie avoided the direct line of their intense, smoky, and hypnotic dreaminess.

He cast her that imperial glance of his that demanded no reproach. "I bought a lot of things after you left."

She frowned. "I thought you didn't like ostentatious things like flashy sports cars."

Shrugging his shoulders, he opened the door, he grabbed a pair of designer sunglasses and slipped them on. The look gave him that mysterious playboy persona, which drove the females wild, no matter their age. "It seems my tastes have changed."

"Apparently," she snapped clenching her teeth.

She slipped into the cool interior of the automobile, clipping her seatbelt. The close confines of the automobile made it hard to stay as far to the right as humanly possible. Even though the glasses shaded his eyes, Maddie retreated under the scrutiny of his arrogant stare. She knew it was arrogant because arrogance was his specialty. But he didn't say anything before starting the car.

As they sped along the road the silence became deafening. Unbearable. Santo could be intimidating if you let him. He was a widely successful business man. He was respected worldwide for his business ingenuity. There wasn't a proposal, or a deal he'd pursued, which he didn't accomplish. His business acumen was globally renowned. Some called him a barracuda in the boardroom. The women called him a vision for the sore eyes.

Yet, the deal that became their marriage was a complete flop. He treated her like unfinished business. The hurt pierced her heart. Their marriage was doomed. They were completely wrong for each other. She had to know the truth. Why he had betrayed her trust. She knew it wasn't smart to dredge up the past, but the deep-seated questions burned deeply within her. She needed to know.

"Why? Why, Santo did you betray me? Sleep with another woman? I was faithful, never betraying our trust."

He turned his head eyeing her through the glass lens. She wished he'd remove them so she could read his eyes. "Really, tesoro. You want to bring up the past and ruin our day?"

"Why do you always avoid the question? I deserve an answer. The only way to heal is getting closure."

Maddie took a deep breath.

"Our only hope for closure, Maddie, is for me to get you out of my system." His flattened lips indicated his irritation.

"A typical answer. Making every conversation about the bedroom," she snapped sharply.

"Very well," he sighed. "I was never unfaithful to you, not while we were together. What you heard and saw weren't true. The child's not mine."

There was a pause. It felt like her heart was being ripped from her chest.

She puffed air in and out concentrating on calm breathing techniques. Her heart twisted and burned as if a knife had pierced her aching chest. Even after all this time he wouldn't admit the truth. He was lying. She knew what she had seen.

"Why, Santo? Why lie to me? I was there. I saw you and Vanessa together. She was in our bed."

It still had the ability to hurt her, crush her.

The moving picture screen flashed through her.

He shoved his glasses onto his head. A brief shadow clouded his face. Regret, but not remorse, pain, or sorrow. A shade of cold, impassiveness, shielded his eyes. The foggy shadows deepened within their cloudy depths. His rugged features seemed frozen in stone. "Believe what you will, Maddie. I won't continue to defend myself." He stared straight ahead at the road, fist clasping the steering wheel. "I've told you the truth. Believe it or not." He shrugged. "I don't care. There's nothing more I can say, or do, to make you believe me."

"But..."

"Enough. This discussion is over."

She wanted to rail at him. Shake her fist in his uncompromising face. Make him feel the hurt that continued to plague her. Make him understand. She knew she wasn't blameless. She'd run, without so much as a word. Avoiding the emotions, the issues, the solutions. All she had ever wanted was his full undivided attention, his love.

"Santo," she pulled the plumb pinkness of her bottom lip between her teeth. "Oh, what's the use.

We're simply incompatible."

His eyes narrowed dangerously. He'd hurt her then, and now. Maybe they were better apart. Why let history repeat itself? He wanted her body, but did he want to contend with all the baggage that came with it. Was it worth it? He wanted to say no, but the stirring in his loins convinced him differently.

"That's not true, Maddie. We are compatible in so many ways," he said softly.

"I know," she exclaimed, "the bedroom," she said, mockery lining her weakened voice.

His serious gaze swept over her ignoring her snide remark. "I intend to enjoy this day. I intend to put the ghosts of our past in the closet. I suggest you do the same."

Then he smiled that sexy, come hither smile, that turned her blood to jelly.

Relax, she told herself. Do that, put the past, just there, in the past. Think about today and the rare opportunity to spend the day with this man who made her quiver with awareness.

She gave him a sunny smile. "You're right. We've got today. Let's make the best of it."

A smile curved his lips, softening his features. "Good."

Although she was pretending to be relaxed

he'd never know.

The city loomed before them. He kept his eyes on the road, maneuvering through the congested traffic. He pulled up before a designer boutique and shut off the engine.

Maddie cringed. "I can't afford this," she told him.

"I'll take care of it."

"No, Santo, I don't want you paying for me. I don't need fancy clothes."

He unhooked his seatbelt, letting it retract back. "Humor me. I enjoy buying you beautiful things."

She cast him a doubtful glance. "Please, let me buy my own."

He nodded. Retracing his actions by hooking the seatbelt back around the broad expanse of his chest. "Fine, if it makes you happy. Where do you want to go?"

"To the little shop I use to frequent," she said. He knew the one. Maddie had always refused to let him dress her. She bought from a second-hand shop. Discontinued designer clothes, at discount prices. He recalled all the times he'd removed the clothes from her luscious, supple body. His body hardened in memory.

He pulled back into the traffic and found the

shop.

Her smile of appreciation pierced his heart. When he made her happy, he felt good inside. He'd always liked making her happy. And simple things did that for her. She didn't need all the things his money could buy. There was nothing superficial about Maddie. She'd grown up in a middle-class family that understood the value of money and money management. He'd never done without material things, but he understood micro management. But money was a tool, and when you were at his earning bracket it was meant to be utilized. Still, Maddie was diligent in her refusal so he let it slide.

She was very precise with her shopping. Targeting the items, she needed, didn't take long. Santo insisted on buying them. To prevent an unnecessary argument, she conceded.

Santo drove her to one of their old haunts to eat, Trattoria Sabatino. A lovely family-owned restaurant that was a favorite to the locals. The food was delicious. Simply Italian.

Maddie recollected the numerous happy times they had come here holding hands, kissing, and so in love. Or so she thought. It had all been an illusion, a figment of her imagination.

She frowned. "Why would you bring me here?"

Santo pulled out her chair, then seated himself. "Why not? You always liked eating here."

"That was back then. Not now."

"Some things never change, amore."

They were interrupted long enough to order their food.

Maddie stared at him. "Ours did, Santo. For the best, don't you think?"

"I liked things how they were," Santo stated. "Now that Nonna passed, it's made me realize we aren't guaranteed anything. My business has been my life, my bed partner. I'm in prime physical condition. I work hard. I play hard. And now I want a son, or daughter, to share it with."

Maddie tugged at her lower lip. That was what all this was about. His grandmother had planted a seed, and Santo decided he wanted it to grow. She was the perfect choice. Still legally his wife, the solution. A pawn in this ugly game he called life.

"Sounds easy, doesn't it?" Maddie unfolded her napkin and laid it on her lap. She raised her eyes, looking at him. He was so self-assured, so smug. "I'm human, not some business portfolio, that you can bend and change to comply with your demands."

"I'm not a monster, Maddie. I won't make you do anything you're not willing to do."

She pulled her lip in between her teeth again and gnawed.

"Quit that," he demanded.

"Quit what?" she wrinkled her nose with con-fusion.

"That," he said when she did it again. He looked at her reddened lip.

"Why?" Maddie quizzed. "I do that all the time."

"I know," Santo replied. "And if you think back," he sighed, "you know what it led to."

Redness flooded her cheeks causing her to press her knees together. Yes, she knew the end result, him replacing her teeth with his, biting, nip-ping, sucking, until she cried out with pleasure. Her eyes darkened with remembered desire.

His gut clenched in response. At that moment he wanted to throw caution to the wind and whisk her to his penthouse apartment and make mad, pas-sionate love to her.

"I want to do that again." His eyes gleamed in response. "Take that soft, tender flesh between my lips until you beg for more."

"Santo," Maddie admonished him. She looked around to see if anyone had heard. Giving a sigh of relief when everyone ignored them. "Don't say things like that."

"Why? It's how I feel. How you make me feel."

"We're in public, for Christ sakes."

"Where's your sense of adventure, tesoro. I remember when we..."

She held up her hand to halt him. "Don't say it. That was a long time ago."

"Was it?" He cast her a dubious smile.

Their food arrived easing the tension. Maddie hadn't been this sexually wired since... since Santo had seduced her all those years ago.

Santo had ordered the Steak Florentine, Maddie the Alfredo. The requested bottle of wine finished off the meal. The place was filling up with a large crowd, so Santo suggested they leave. Maddie agreed.

"Thank you," Maddie said, once they were back in the car. "The meal was great."

"And the company," he gave her a teasing glance before putting his glasses back on.

"The company had a lot to be desired," she teased him in return.

"Touché," he said, bringing the engine to life.

Those few minutes of relaxed congenial comradery felt great.

Maddie gazed out the window at the passing scenery when they left the city behind. He stopped the car in front of the villa, then took her hand and wove through the massive gardens.

"Where are we going?" she asked puzzled.

"You'll see," is all he said.

He continued walking until they reached the helipad. The helicopter gleamed under the brilliant sun. Barrella Enterprises was inscribed on the side. Santo pulled open the door and helped her inside.

Maddie smiled, but was confused. She loved to fly. This had been their mode of transportation many times, in the past, for business trips. She put on her headset and buckled the seatbelt. Santo climbed into the other side. She looked around for the pilot, but no one was present.

"Where's the pilot?"

"We don't need one," Santo explained. "I'm going to fly this beast."

Maddie cast him a super surprised glance. In the past he'd never flown it himself. She didn't even know he had a pilot's license. But then she didn't know a lot of things about him.

"You can fly this," her voice sounded a bit doubtful.

"Don't worry," he patted her knee. "You'll be safe."

The engine roared to life. The blades whirled noisily above them. Santo adjusted the necessary controls, then lifted the powerful machine into the air. The sound was almost deafening.

She was still curious as to their destination. Italy from the sky was like a patchwork quilt, masses of rolling green hills. She leaned over and looked at the beautiful scenery spread out below. Her heart fluttered with joy. She should've become a pilot, she thought, it was so empowering. She smiled at Santo, he smiled back.

Maddie leaned back and enjoyed the flight. She leaned forward when the turquoise blue waters of the Mediterranean came into view. Once they landed he came around and helped her from the beast of a machine. She stepped out, and he caught her in his arms. She caught her lip, and he groaned. She loved having that power over him. The power to make him want her sexually. And he did want her, his eyes were sending definite arousing messages.

Before she could speak, he took her arm and guided her to a waiting car. The driver held the door for them to climb into the back seat. The lush interior was cool and the plush, luxurious black leather seats wrapped around her form.

Once settled, Maddie turned to him again. "Where are we going?"

His brilliant even white teeth flashed when he smiled. Her heart tap danced. "Somewhere quiet and special." And that's all he would say.

She slid back onto the plush, leather seat and waited. She'd know soon enough.

The car pulled up along the coastline before a magnificent yacht. Maddie cast him a curious glance, but he still didn't respond. His eyelashes shielded his eyes, revealing nothing.

"Come on," he ordered. He took her hand and helped her from the car. The driver pulled away leaving the two of them alone.

"Did you rent this, or what?" Maddie stood amazed eyeing the beauty of the boat.

"No." He pulled her along. The staff quickly welcomed him aboard.

Then she saw it. The beautiful, scripted letters across the luxury yacht, Maddie, was inscribed with gold letters.

She stopped in her tracks. She couldn't believe her eyes. She threw him an astounded, puzzled look. Her mouth gaped open. She didn't know rather to mad or happy. Honored or dishonored. What game was he playing now?

"Do you like it?" was all he said.

"Santo, what is this? Why?" Tears beaded in her widened eyes.

He placed his hand on the small of her back and ushered her down the steps. Once below he answered. "I commissioned it when you were here, but you left. My gift to you. Sorry it's so late."

She swallowed several times trying to get past the lump in her throat. "I don't understand. Why?" Tears trickled from beneath her lashes even when she tried to hold them back.

The pad of his thumb swiped away a tear. "Because," he whispered against her hair, "I cared about you. I wanted to please you, amore mio." Past tense.

She shivered from his touch. "It's beautiful, but gifts weren't what I wanted. I wanted you."

"You have me," he said, brushing the curls from her face. "I'm right here. Give me a chance to make it up to you. Trust me."

She looked up, her steady gaze holding his. "That's rich coming from you. Why read more into this than there is? I want you, I'll give you that, but trust."
The lingering demons of their past haunted her. She couldn't get past it.

She tugged on her lip again. He groaned, yanking her taunt form into his. His mouth captured hers, his tongue gaining entry, dueling with hers. The moist weapon darted against hers. He held nothing back. His lips bruised hers while his tongue stroked, took, and demanded her equally rewarding response.

He finally stopped when they both needed air.

He tore his mouth from hers. She panted. Both of their breathing was ragged. Hot and bothered barely described the feelings rushing through her. Her body fueled by his scorching touch.

She shifted beneath his hooded gaze. She knew she was risking her heart to him, but she didn't have the power to stop it. Women were programed to want so much more than physical satisfaction alone. They wanted the emotions, the feelings, the happily ever after. She had to guard herself from those types of emotions. So, she stood there, the expressions on her face giving away all the hunger her body craved. His chest puffed out and heaved with his quick intake of air. His smile was arrogant and satisfied.

He knew, in that moment, he'd gained her complete surrender. This grown up game of sexual prowess was nothing but physical. She wanted it. He wanted it. So why not answer their basic needs. After all, they were married. This is what married couples engage in, sexual gratification. That little nagging voice reminding her she wanted more was cast aside.

She'd iron out all the emotional stuff later, but right now she wanted him.

Her voice trembled with need. "Santo." And that was all the invitation he needed. He swept her back into his arms.

"I want you Maddie. I've always wanted you."
His eyes held a solemn promise. "I thought this
burning need for you had gone out a long time ago,
but it hasn't. Please, come to my bed and quench
this thirst I have for you."

Chapter 6

In that moment her surroundings faded from view. The super yacht and all its opulence became blurred. She focused on his rugged, handsome face. Her chest heaved. His eyes honed in and locked with hers.

Her breath felt labored.

She wanted to look away, but there was nowhere else she'd rather look. He mesmerized her. She was his captive audience. Her unwillingness a poor substitute.

One perfected grey look, enticed her.

His fingers brushed the underside of her breast. She gasped. His taste lingered on her lips. His touch burned in her memory. He was hell bent on breaking down her resistance. He didn't need to work very hard at it.

His hand moved to her shoulder, then clasped her neck, pulling her toward him.

"You look so innocent," he whispered, "like the virgin I touched for the first time so long ago. Timid, frightened, yet, so willing to explore all the mysteries I'm so willing to share. But, you know those mysteries, sweet, Maddie. We have explored them all before. Let me show you all over again."

Her eyes fluttered shut. His soft, coaxing voice was like magic. Hypnotizing her, pulling her into his trance. Her head rolled back, her hair cascaded down her spine, and she moistened her lips. Sweet, torturous memories. All of her sensory vibes were on high alert.

"Santo," she said, brokenly. Need evident in the sound of her voice.

His mouth found hers. Their tongues tangoed increasing the eroticism of their touch. He pulled back, she felt deprived. Suddenly he picked her up, cradling her sensitized body against his, and carried her to the bedroom.

She tried to protest, but couldn't, wouldn't. The jumbled words came out a needful moan.

Maddie briefly saw her surroundings as he placed her on the bed. The room was decorated with turquoise blue, her favorite color. His attention to detail caused her heart to skip a beat. He'd thought of her every need, her every comfort, when commissioning this boat. Had he cared?

But, then, he was there, beside her, running his hands along her erogenous zones. The ripples of primal awareness consumed her. She moaned with pleasure. His clothes were gone. He was naked. She clasped his shoulders. She kneaded his back. He found the zip on her dress. She wiggled, giving him better access, the zip parted. He pulled the obtrusive fabric from her frame and tossed it to the floor. It had been so long. So, long. This man, her husband, never failed to please her sexually.

He raised onto his forearms. His unfathomable eyes gleamed. "Maddie," he moaned, his voice brimming with desire. "I've wanted this for so long."

"Me too," she said, cupping her hands against his cheeks. "Make love to me."

He needed no further prompting. He nipped at the pulse pounding in her neck. His hands explored her supple flesh. Oh, so quickly, his fingers found a path of remembrance. He pushed her hair away from her face, kissing her cheek, her eyelids, her nose, and then her lips.

His hand cupped the ripe, fullness of her breast. Massaging, kneading, pinching the engorged nipple between his fingertips. Maddie tried to stay calm despite the heady combination of his exacerbating touch.

She clawed his shoulders, his back, knowing she was leaving her mark.

She arched her hips, her thighs spreading apart, allowing him entry to her most private part. His breathing became rapid. He plundered one breast and then the other. Her feet planted in the mattress the pleasure almost unbearable. He nuzzled her neck, biting her erratic pulse that pounded furiously. Greedily, she pressed her lips to his jaw. Follow-

ing the line to his ear, sucking the lobe between
her teeth, licking the cavern with her tongue. He
groaned, causing her intense joy. He positioned his
aroused length against her entrance.
She accommodated him by widening her thighs further.
His hands continued to roam her flushed, moist
body. The foreplay was nearly her undoing.
"Take me, Santo. Please," she begged.
And then he entered her. He hovered above her increasing the anticipation. And then he moved slowly
at first then harder and faster. She nearly climaxed
from his smooth touch. She bit her lip, she panted,
as the friction increased. It about took her breath
away. He increased his tempo, she met his rhythm.
Suddenly she forgot all the pain, all the reasons she'd
ever left. This pleasure blotted out everything except fulfillment.
His penetration got deeper and deeper. She wanted
this to last forever. To never end. It felt so good.
So right. She felt the pinnacle of her desire building,
reaching its limit.
She cried out his name and held on tight as the explosion sent orgasmic tremors flying though her. He
caught her moan in his mouth as his movements became more urgent. She knew he was on the brink as
her convulsions surrounded him. Her moan became

his. He jerked with his own powerful explosion. She exhaled her pleasure heady with the power she had over him. In that moment of sexual fulfillment, he was completely hers.

They lay depleted.

He kissed her neck. Their mingled sweat filmed her body.

A single tear trickled down her cheek. Not because of pain, but pleasure. It was too good, better than she remembered. Memory was no comparison to reality.

He rolled to her side, pulling her into his arms. "Maddie."

She brushed his hair from his forehead. "Thank you," was all she could manage.

"The pleasure was all mine."

He cradled her face between his palms and gently kissed her. It was sweet, endearing, and caring. Did they have a chance? Was it possible to mend their broken marriage?

She was being foolish. Dredging up feelings that were fledging emotions, false hopes, this had been nothing but great sex.

Her mind was swimming with what ifs and what now.

She pulled away and laid her head on the other pillow. He rose upon an elbow, the sheet barely covering his hip. Maddie quickly adverted her gaze away, his body pooling awareness back to her center. She clamped her knees together as if that would make it go away.

He smiled knowingly.

His smile was torment. She couldn't resist it. She was a strong, independent woman, driven, but his dark sensuality never failed to entrap her. She'd just committed treason. Resistance was no longer a viable option.

His fingers traced along her arm, stopping, tickling her wrist. The whisper of his touch caused shivers and goosebumps to quiver upon her skin. She trembles to the sensation her muscles clenching deeply inside her. The vibrations of his vibrant touch sent her into a frenzy of raw emotions.

She knew what he wanted, round two.

His grey eyes of molten steel begged for her acceptance.

Maddie turned away, ignoring the powerful urge to agree.

"Why did you choose this color?" She waved her hand indicating the room.

He settled deeper into the mattress. "It's your favorite color." He shrugged his bare shoulder, causing her to quickly look away.

"How did you know that? Did I tell you?" She

racked her memory bank, trying to remember.
He leaned back against the stark, white sheets,
clamping his hands behind his head. The sheet slid
further down, exposing parts that she couldn't bear
to look at without losing control. He tugged the
sheet up and chuckled, causing her further discomfort.
 "I know a lot of things about you, Signora Barrella,"
his sumptuous voice said.
Her head swiveled toward him. "What do you mean?
Like what?"
"Like the sensuous way you pull your bottom lip between your teeth when you're nervous or turned on."
She unconsciously proved him right. He honed in on
the lip she bit. "The way you purr like a kitten when
you sleep." He wrapped her wayward curl around his
finger. Playing with her hair as he spoke. "The way
your eyes shimmer with flecks of gold when you're
angry. The way you look at me when you think I
don't notice."
She held up her hand, stopping him. "Okay, I got it.
So, you picked up on my weakened attributes."
He shook his head. "I love all your little quirks. It
makes you the person you are, the person you've
become."
Her politely enquiring expression flew over his superb body sublimely reclined against the headboard.

His eyes were partially closed and relaxed.
Their eyes locked and held.
Hurt temporarily filled her eyes. He felt a moment's regret, a twinge of sorrow.
"You can pepper me with your pretty words, Santo, but this is sex, nothing more. It solves nothing. I caved under your seductive skills. It won't happen again."
"Won't it?" He rose from the bed, his glorious body on full display.
Her cheeks tinted pink, but she couldn't look away.
"Yes," she promised softly. "I can't." She was trying to hold back the pain, the bitterness. "I won't continue a relationship based upon nothing but physical intimacy and nothing else."
She was struggling to remain stern, focused, with his naked body displayed so unabashedly right before her.
"Please, Santo, put some clothes on," she said.
"Why, amore mio," he snickered, "am I distracting you?"
His semi-erection became hard. Her breathing shallowed. It was no use because neither of them could resist the temptation against their mutual attraction. He climbed back in the bed, his mouth found and plundered hers.
The madness started all over again.

Maddie groaned her inner most pleasure and ran her fingernails across his skin. He panted and gasped. The sound sent muscles spasms crashing straight to her nether regions. Moist heat greedily filled the space between her thighs. "Oh, my beautiful Maddie," it was a half cry and half moan.
 She was panting, matching him kiss for kiss and touch for touch. His hands were everywhere gliding along every sensitized contour. She reciprocated branding him with her commanding imprint. Her tortured breathing equaled his. The complexity of their kisses increased. Hunger consumed them. Their pace amplified as they headed toward the finish line. She felt her body exploding, unraveling beneath him. She panted, she groaned and cried out his name until the fiery combustive explosion erupted. Santo cried out her name. Her body was enslaved by his consuming touch. Legs wrapped around him she smiled her pleasure. She kissed his lips. The first time was full of pent up need, but this time was different, so carnal, so necessary and so fulfilling.
It was a long while before they came back to their senses. She had completely forfeited her hard-earned stripes.
Santo's eyes narrowed. Her reddened lips, her puckered pink nipples, and tousled hair were signs of a

woman who'd been completely sated.

He rubbed his thumb against her tender nipple and heard her sigh. His jaw clenched and his voice came out in a rasp. "My sweet, Maddie, so responsive," he said. "Now that you're in my bed, you'll stay. I promise."

She started to protest, but he rose and walked into the bathroom. She heard the spray of the shower, then closed her eyes.

***

Maddie awoke from a deep sleep, groggy and confused. Where was she? Then the memories came crashing back.

The space beside her was empty. There was no sign of Santo.

She rose up stiff from her recent activity. But she felt sated and torn.

She smiled in spite of herself.

Why not? There was nothing like making love to your husband, even an absent partner.

She stretched and yawned, kicking the sex scented sheets away from her naked body.

She was replete and satisfied. All indications of a woman falling in love.

Where had that come from? It caused a jagged bolt of electricity to slash at her heart.

She looked at the indention of the pillow lying beside her. She couldn't resist, pulling it to her chest, she inhaled his scent into her nostrils.
That's how he found her.
Maddie guiltily tossed the pillow to the side.
His eyes glinted, and he smiled knowingly. He carried a tray of food. He moved to the bedside and placed the tray down.
His eyes darkened as he took in her lush, replete, body. Maddie tucked the sheet tighter. Although it was a little late for modesty.
"I thought you might be hungry," he smiled. "Strenuous exercise always makes me hungry."
She blushed. Even after all their familiarity she still blushed like a school girl. The smell made her stomach rumble rebelliously.
"Eat," he instructed.
She picked up the glass and drank the cool, refreshing water.
"Here," he handed her a piece of bread slathered with butter.
"Thanks," she said, taking it and raising it to her mouth. He stood watching her making it hard to relax.
Santo was casually dressed. His white T-shirt accentuated his dark skin. The shorts exposed his muscular calves.

"I'm sorry I fell asleep," she apologized. "How long did I sleep?"
He shrugged. "Probably an hour."
She cringed. "Really. I can't believe it."
"He sat on the edge of the bed. His hand upon her thigh. "You needed the rest. You've looked really tired lately."
His nearness was making it hard to focus. "I need to shower and dress." She looked around at her scattered clothes on the floor.
"Yeah, sure," Santo agreed. "Everything you need is in there."
He pointed to a door adjacent to the bed. He rose. "I'll meet you on deck in a bit."
She nodded avoiding his eyes.
As soon as he left she scrambled out of the bed. Wrapping the sheet around her nakedness.
Opening the door, she found a huge closet filled with everything she'd possibly need. Her first thought was how many women had he brought here. How many had worn these clothes?
Running her fingers along the line of hangers she knew they were intended for her. She wondered when he'd done all this. The clothes were the latest styles and designs.
Pulling a blouse from the hanger she then found a pair of shorts and sandals. The drawers were filled

with silky, sexy underwear, that she felt hesitant to wear. But what choice did she have.

The huge shower with numerous water jets sprayed against her skin. The water soothed her aching muscles. The water slightly stung her skin. Closing her eyes, Maddie shampooed her hair, and then, felt for the towel.

Her hand encountered his, the towel dangling from his fingertips. Her eyes popped open. His desire filled eyes were clamped on the beads of water splayed upon her skin.

She crisscrossed her arms against her breasts, sheltering them from his view.

Heat pooled between her legs. Seductive intent filled his heated eyes.

He dropped the towel and stepped into the spraying water.

Maddie gulped. "Your clothes," she said, "they're soaked."

"A small price to pay," he uttered, pulling her into his arms.

Her head rolled back, exposing the arch of her neck to his burning lips. He suckled the raging pulse beneath his mouth. His hands were everywhere. Her hot, Italian husband, was insatiable.

Sanity eluded her. She wanted this man's body so much. She raked her tongue against his. Boldness

drove her every move. She pressed her body against his, wrapping her arms around his neck. Her fingers raked through his dark, wet hair. The tempo of their breathing steadily increased. Her purring, kitten sounds, rose from her throat.
His lips rained a burning trail of fire along her neck, to her shoulder, then clamped her breast. He shoved his erection hard against her. He hands clamped her wet buttocks, squeezing the rounded flesh. Desperate need drove him void of any rational thought. His usual finesse deserted him as an overpowering need to be inside her consumed him. He couldn't think except about the way she tasted.
She moaned, she groaned, her knees nearly buckled. His clothes were a barrier. He let her go to shed his wet clothes. And then he was naked. The fire inside him burned hotly. He dipped his hand between her legs rubbing the pad of his thumb against the heated nub. She gasped, arching her back. An added invitation to continue.
"Oh my, oh my," she chanted, as he slowly, meticulously brought her to completion.
Her climax was explosive. Overpowering. She clamped his shoulders and rode out the storm.
He was holding back his release. He was so close to the edge. He let her ride out her pleasure before gaining his own. "I need you Maddie. I have to be

inside you."
And then with practiced, gentle care he entered her.
His climax soon followed.
Together they leaned against the slick tiles. Their
breathing labored as their heartbeats decreased its
rhythm.
Maddie opened her eyes and looked at his black, wet
hair, plastered against her chest.
What the hell had just happened? She'd lost com-
plete control.
He stepped back his smile of satisfaction curved upon
his lips. He twisted the knobs stopping the water.
"I'm sorry," he apologized. "Your wet, soapy body
was too much for me to resist."
She lowered her eyes, regaining her composure.
"There is nothing to be sorry for. I couldn't resist
you, either."
"Lust is a powerful thing."
His words hurt. Leave it to Santo to call what they
done, been doing, lust.
No endearing words of love, commitment, or compassion.
Maddie exited the shower and picked up the fluffy,
white towel that had been discarded earlier. She
wrapped it tightly around her.
Santo's nakedness was boldly on display, and he
didn't hurry to cover himself. His boldness suddenly

irritated her. She was frazzled and frustrated while he remained a stoic tower of confidence.

The silence stretched between them.

He found a towel and dried his black hair and then his glorious body. Maddie averted her hungry gaze. How could she still crave his body after their numerous bouts of lovemaking? She hadn't thought she'd become insatiable. Was she crazy?

Wrapping the towel around his waist, he picked up his scattered, wet clothes off the floor.

Maddie slipped into the clothes she'd laid on the bed. She inhaled and exhaled several times to calm her frazzled nerves. She regained her confidence once dressed.

Santo dropped the towel when he entered the closet. Maddie's eyes encompassed his tight, firm, round buttock before spinning around.

This day hadn't turned out anything like she had planned.

Maddie jumped when his fingers skated along her quivering flesh.

"Come," he held out his hand, "let me show you your namesake."

Tentatively she placed her hand in his. His eyes were fathomless, unreadable. While hers reflected uncertainty.

He led her up the steps to the deck. The brightness

of the sun caused her to squint. The boat moved nearly motionless upon the azure blue of the Mediterranean Sea.

Santo intertwined their fingers as he pulled her to the edge of the gleaming, super powered vessel. Instead of her namesake, it should've been his. It mimicked his power, his strength, and beauty. It embodied all things related to Santo and his massive empire. But all the wealth in the world meant nothing without happiness. It left emptiness.

"What do you think?" He waited for her response.

What was she supposed to say? The yacht itself, was absolutely stunning. It embodied all the elements money could buy.

She smiled prettily. "It's beautiful, Santo. I'm speechless you would have named it after me. Why did you?"

He shielded his eyes with his hand, propping his elbows on the edge and shrugged. "It seemed right at the time. You were my wife."

His words felt like a gut punch. "I still am," she added.

"Are you?" His mouth hardened. "I'm not convinced, tesoro. We have a piece of paper saying such, but it means nothing. You've changed, Maddie. You're withholding part of yourself."

She clasped the railing, her fists clenched around the

heated metal. She'd just had hot, sizzling sex with him all afternoon. They had fantastic sex, but they still had a failed marriage. He'd reiterated the fact. The faith she'd had in him so long ago was now just a distant memory.

It was stupid. No use travelling down that sentimental journey of ugly memories. Her vulnerability was surfacing. In the two years of separation she'd built a wall of protection around herself. She thought she had become a different woman, secure in her beliefs. Yet, in one day, he laid claim to her body and the outer ridges of her heart.

"You're right," she spoke boldly. "I'm not the young, selfless woman you married. You enrolled me into the school of hard knocks. Lesson learned," she assured him. "I'm sorry, Santo, but I can never be that girl again."

He shifted slightly. A brief shadow of sadness passed through his eyes, but was gone as quickly, that she might have imagined it.

She wondered, did he regret hurting her.

He shook his head. "I think we both know what we had is finished. We travelled that road, and I don't want to go back. The past is over, and we can't change it." The scowl on his rugged features deepened. "Quit reading more into this than there is. Accept it for what it is, and let us move forward."

"What do you want," she snapped. "For me to fall into your bed whenever you snap your fingers."

His eyes narrowed into angry slits. "Careful, Maddie. You were as willing as I. The thread of attraction between us is mutual."

Her heart pounded. "Sex doesn't solve anything."

"Doesn't it," he laughed. "I wondered if you were as good as I remembered. And you are. You're a great lover. And we both wanted it. I don't see the harm in satisfying our needs."

She'd take the blame for giving him the ammunition to hurt her. She'd fallen into his ruthless trap, again. What a fool she was.

She licked her dry lips. She suddenly felt horrible. All the closeness they'd just shared now felt wrong somehow.

"I'm not your mistress, or friend with benefits. I'm your wife," Maddie said. "Doesn't the sanctity of marriage mean anything to you?"

Suddenly what they'd shared seemed dirty.

He ran his fingers through his hair and grinned. "Se. Don't turn this into something it's not. You left the marriage sanctity a long time ago. I want you. Isn't that enough?"

His eyes zeroed in on her. Resentment filled her eyes.

He turned and walked away and left her standing alone. Unwanted tears clouded her eyes as she watched his retreating back. She leaned back against the railing, worrying her lip between her teeth. She closed her eyes briefly before looking up at the cumulus clouds dotting the purest blue sky, imploring the heavens for an answer as to why she was suffering this punishment. He'd put the fire back in her only to pull it back out.

Chapter 7

Decision made. He turned off the lights and locked the door.

She didn't know him. It was time to change that. Show her the side of him that mattered. No more waiting. Tonight, he would reclaim his wife, physically, mentally, and eThe first rule of ending a marriage to divorce is don't fall into the same trap twice.

Or three times.

Maddie stared at the endless expanse of blue that surrounded her. She stood frozen on the spot. A series of emotions charged through her, hurt, anger, then back to hurt.

She'd known their racing hormones, raging desires, weren't the answer. She had the makings of a roaring headache. She rubbed her temples and sighed.

"Excuse me, signora, but Signor Barrella asks that you join him below."

Maddie turned to find the staff member addressing her.

"Please," he indicated the steps from where she had come.

"Thank you," she nodded and followed him below.

She spotted Santo standing at the teakwood

bar, tossing back a drink. A thousand questions swirled through her mind. She wanted to understand his motivations, his reasons, for dragging her here today. Making love to her and then tossing it back in her face. She wasn't his wife, she was his plaything. Someone he wanted to toy with until he grew tired of her like he'd done before.

He poured his glass three fingers full and tossed it back. She frowned, Santo never drank hard liquor, only wine.

She remembered the first time she had met him, oh, so long ago. Her heart had melted the first time he spoke to her. She had been enraptured with his classic, chiseled good looks.

He had pursued her relentlessly. She had been thrilled from the chase. He hadn't needed to try too hard. She'd been willing from the beginning. Captured by his smile. Captured by his touch.

She had fallen fast and hard.

So, when the betrayal had come, she'd been broken. Shattered into a million tiny pieces.

It had taken her months, years to mend. Apparently, she never had. As soon as she saw him, grief stricken over his grandmother, all the hurt had rushed back. She'd felt battered all over again.

She wanted to pommel his smooth, hard chest and take all the years of misery and frustration out on him. Make him feel her pain, her hurt, her sorrow.

She waited for him to turn and face her, but he didn't. He knew she was there. His broad shoulders were taunt with tension.

Reconciliation's were supposed to be joyful, happy.

Theirs was the exact opposite.

"Santo, say something." She waited for his response.

He turned slowly. His eyes were that steely grey that made him a worthy adversary.
Strong, powerful, and impossible to beat.

She refused to lower her eyes or give him a hint of her timidity.

When a lion's prey, you never let him know you were scared or nervous.

And she wasn't, not really.

"I'm sorry," he said simply.

Maddie's eyes widened with surprise. She hadn't expected an apology.

She waited.

He stepped toward her, then changed his mind. "I'm sorry I hurt you. I'm sorry I married you and then betrayed your trust. And," he paused, "I'm sorry I ever let you leave my bed."

Leave it to Santo to ruin a perfectly good apology.

She shook her head. "Sorry isn't always enough," she said. "I'm sorry I ever climbed into your bed. If I hadn't then this vicious cycle would be so much easier to break."

He clenched his jaw and his lips compressed into a thin line of disapproval. "I thought," he continued, "if we had sex it would appease this unbearable itch I have for you. But I was wrong."

"What?"

"Instead of curbing my hunger for you, I want more. I have a voracious appetite, amore."

Hurt clenched at her chest. "It's always about sex with you, isn't it?

"Sex is a relative term," he said. "You're right," he smiled crookedly, finally agreeing with something she'd said. "It's about your beautiful body and welcoming smile."

She frowned her annoyance.

"I love to banter with you. You're very graceful, Maddie, and very smart. I like to be challenged not only in the bedroom, but outside it too."

He sat down his unfinished glass of liquid. He came toward her, she stepped back. His eyes narrowed. Her retreat was automatic protection. Her tension mounted.

"Come," he held out his hand, "we need to

eat."

She eyed his hand but refused to take it. Instinct warned her not to touch him again.
He nodded, dropping his hand back to his side.

"After you," he said. Pointing in the direction
of the fragrant smell of food.

He pulled out a chair tucked beneath the can-
dlelit table covered by a sparkling white tablecloth.
She took a seat. His hand brushed her shoulder,
intentionally or accidentally, who knows, still she
shuttered.

He moved around the table and took his seat.

"Wine," he lifted his brow in question.

She tilted her glass, biting the corner of her
lip, then quickly stopped when his gaze darkened
responsively.

Her little tell-tale habit was a turn on. She
must learn to break that habit.

They were served several courses, she barely took a bite from each. She concentrated on the
wine, sipping gingerly, hoping to calm her nerves.
How this man, who she'd shared every possible intimacy, could make her so hot and bothered, was a
mystery.

He rose from the table. "Come," he told her.
"It's time to go."

Just like that he was back in control. No emotions. No desire, strictly control. His darkened eyes reflected nothing.

While her eyes were full of hunger, want, need, and sorrow.

Their day full of intimacy had ended. His abruptness was aggravating.

When they climbed topside day had turned into night, and a blanket of stars twinkled in the black sky. The boat was coming around to the shore. They'd docked, and the boardwalk was well lit below. He strode across the deck and exited the boat, leaving her to follow.

Maddie was confused. Now what? One minute he was hot, then cold. What had angered him? She'd never understand his moodiness. His never explaining himself left her feeling deprived.

The car was waiting where it had left them. He opened her door, closing it after she slipped inside. He climbed in beside her, but not a word was spoken, silence reigned within the enclosed space. His stern jaw was clenched. His fingers drummed on his thigh. She took his cue and directed her attention out the window. She stared at nothing except darkness.

His phone rang, startling in the silence, causing her to jump.

He spoke in rapid Italian, leaving her to guess

who was on the phone. His frown only deepened. Whoever it was, he wasn't happy.

The helicopter waited. He helped her inside, but this time, he didn't pilot the machine. Her nerves were stretched as tight as a bow string, he still didn't say a word.

The flight was quick but seemed endless. Once landed he helped her out. She mutely followed him inside. He left her standing. Strode from the room. She needed to move but was frozen to the spot. She was still standing, her eyes haunted, when he returned.

He had changed. His dark pants and jacket accentuating his olive skin.

"I've got to go," he said, stiffly. "I'm not sure when I'll return. Relax. Enjoy your stay."

"Fine," she inhaled deeply, outrage flooding her cheeks with color. "That's it, you tumble me on the sheets, make love to me, drop me off, and say goodbye."

"Nothing personal. Business, I must attend to," he responded sagely.

Her hands clenched into fists. "I didn't sign on for this, Santo. I came here for your grandmother, nothing more. I'm sorry I didn't divorce you a long time ago," she cried softly.

He cursed. He marched toward her stopping mere inches away. "Heed my words, tesoro. Divorce is off the table. This marriage stays intact until I say otherwise. Capisce."

She glared at him in defiance, her breathing measured. "Don't ever...tell me what to do. I'll decide for myself."

With that she stomped away, leaving him in a cloud of fury.

. . .

Santo's anger knew no bounds. She'd defied him. Inexcusable. He wanted to follow her and claim her willing body and demand her compliance, but he had to go. Pressing matters required his immediate attention.

Maddie had become more headstrong and independent, maybe she always had been. She was full of combustible fire. He cursed. If he was honest, only increased his desire. Seeing her mad as hell sent the blood crashing to his groin. He was fully turned on.

Since when had he allowed a woman the power to make him think with certain body parts, instead of his brain? He needed a cold shower.

A lapse in judgment.

He stormed from the room, adrenalin urging him forward.

Since the first moment he'd met her, his brain

power had been disengaged. She did that to him, made him lose control. He didn't like the feeling. When she'd left him two years ago he'd cried like a baby and drank himself into a stupor. Nonna had demanded he go after her, but he had refused.

The pain, from that memory, still had the ability to make him suffer.

He looked at his phone screen, wanting to call her, but shoved it back into his pocket. What he wanted to say shouldn't be said on the phone, but in person.

He wanted to see her eyes, touch her lips, when he reclaimed her.

His muscles clenched with desire when he thought of their day. His body should've been sated, but he still craved her touch.

The car cruised into the city lights, Santo instructed the driver to stop at a bustling nightclub. In his current mood he'd no tolerance for nonsense and Marco, his best friend, always caused him prob- lems. This time would be no different.

As he stepped from the confines of the vehicle he could hear the sounds of the pounding music from within. This wasn't his scene, nor did he like to come here, but necessity dictated it. Florence's most glamorous, ultra-chic space was glowing with neon blue hues, and the dance floor was crowded with stylish dancers gyrating to the music.

Santo's head began to pound with the music. He felt so out of place. He'd never been a clubber even as a twenty-something.

His eyes squinted in the dim, blue atmosphere. Then he saw him, dirty dancing with a willing partner. Marco, a constant thorn in his side.

As he wove through the crowd several prying hands and lewd comments were thrown his way. He ignored them and frowned. Marco had gotten him into these situations too many times to count.

As a matter of fact, it was Marco who'd brought an end to his marriage, because of his inconceivable stupidity.

He inhaled and exhaled as he continued to push away unwanted advances.

Then, Marco saw him, and laughed. Santo was a storm cloud full of displeasure.

"Santo," he shouted, above the noise. "Nice to see you."

"Marco," Santo hissed.

"Did you come to join me? About time," he laughed again.

Santo's eyes narrowed in frustration. Marco was loaded. He'd probably be forced to carry him out.

"Excuse me, sugar." Santo pried the clinging

vine from Marco's chest. She didn't resist when see-ing his face. She hurried away.

"Hey," Marco complained.

"Marco," Santo continued, "it's time to go."

Marco laughed again. "You're always the bul-ly, Santo. Relax. Enjoy life sometimes."

"No thanks. We need to go."

Slapping him on the shoulder, Marco com-plied. Thankfully he proceeded before him to the door.

Santo took several gulps of fresh air once they were outside. He opened the car door and motioned for Marco to get inside. Marco obeyed for once.

Santo made his way around and climbed in.

"What's got you so ticked?" Marco asked.

Santo gave him a sidelined glance. "Did you ever think it might be you?"

Marco threw him a charismatic grin that got him into more trouble than good. "Possibly," he said, "but it's more than me. So, what gives?"

"Nothing that concerns you."

But in Marco's inebriated condition he pressed for more. "Come on, Santo. I've known you for a long time and something is seriously bothering you."

"It's nothing."

Marco leaned forward and looked at his sol-emn expression. "Oh, my God, it's a woman."

"The reason I'm here, Marco, isn't to discuss me, but you. Vanessa called."

Marco groaned. "Of course, she did."

"Marco you need to stop this unacceptable behavior. How many times have I bailed you out of these situations. "Dio, you have a son. Grow up, take responsibility for your actions."

"I married Vanessa, didn't I? She's intolerable. All she ever wanted was you, Santo."

Santo cringed.   Briefly he saw the hurt shadow Marco's face.

Santo had dated Vanessa a few times. Nothing serious. Marco had been smitten with her almost immediately. Santo knew and ended his association with Vanessa.

But, Marco and Vanessa had been incompatible, tumultuous. They dated, but Marco couldn't remain faithful, nor Vanessa. Then, Vanessa had become pregnant. The relationship deteriorated.

When Maddie had found them together, it had been a mistake. Vanessa had contrived a plan to break up Santo's marriage. She succeeded.

On that fateful night she had climbed into his bed, when he was sleeping. She'd stolen Marco's key to Santo's city apartment.

And that's how Maddie had found them, Vanessa in his bed naked, blaming him for her pregnancy.

He'd slept with her, but only once, and before Maddie.

The memories of that day kept crashing around him. The deceit and hurt ever present.

He knew the child wasn't his, he'd done the testing to prove it.

Maddie wouldn't listen, still wouldn't. The child definitely belonged to Marco.

Vanessa's actions had destroyed so much. Santo's marriage. Marco's life, along with that of his family. Marco buried his hurt in drink.

Marco still loved Vanessa. It was plain.

Santo shook his head. Snapping out of the cloudy memories.

"Marco, go home to your family. Tell your wife you love her, get help, make it work."

"Oh, that's rich, Santo. I sit beside a man who has mourned his wife for two years and refuses to make amends. If it's so easy why haven't you taken your own advice?"

Santo refused to respond.

Marco chuckled. "Same old Santo. Close-mouthed when it comes to your affairs, huh?" He leaned forward, holding Santo's gaze. "How is Maddie?"

Santo threw him a startled glance.

"Don't act surprised, Santo. I know she's here, at the villa."

"How?" Santo snapped.

Marco arched his brow. "She's gotten to you, again, hasn't she? Maddie always was your match." Santo ran his fingers through his hair and looked away. "I don't know what you're talking about. You're drunk."

"Not that drunk," Marco said. "Like I said take your own advice, go home, claim your wife, and leave me the hell alone."

Santo knew it was the alcohol talking, or he would have ended his friendship with Marco right then. No one talked to Santo like that and got away with it. Friend or foe.

Santo left Marco at his door and drove away without saying another word. His apartment was not far away so he found himself there. Opening the door, he switched on the lights and looked around at the masculine space. So many bad memories came rushing in. Was Marco, right? Was he being a hyp-ocrite? He threw out advice but was so unwilling to take it.

He looked around. He should've gotten rid of this place a long time ago. Maddie would never want to spend time there. It held nothing but heart-ache for her. He made a decision to contact a realtor and put the place on the market. He'd find another. Something Maddie wanted. They would search together as a couple.

Marco, as bad as he hated to admit it, was right. He should tell Maddie the truth once and for all. She deserved his honest confession of good faith. He roamed about the sterile space and cringed with misgivings. So much wasted time had passed. He craved his wife with too much pent-up passion. Their time on the boat hadn't even begun to appease his lust. His body hardened with need.

Chapter 8

Maddie tossed and turned, finally giving up on sleep. Santo hadn't returned, or she hadn't heard him. She was still furious that he had the audacity to order her around.

She might have allowed it once, but not now.

She couldn't process any of her jumbled thoughts. They swirled like a plague around and around in her clouded mind.

Leaving her room, she went to the kitchen and stumbled through the dark. Running her hand along the wall she found the light switch. Flipping it on, she jumped.

He sat, in the dark, head in hands. The earlier chemistry slid through her veins. He was so beautiful, sitting there all alone. She wanted to rush over to him and kiss him. Tell him she was sorry. But she didn't. If she were honest, she wanted to be close to him. The natural bond shared between husband and wife was hard to break, especially when she didn't want to.

"Santo," she said tentatively, expecting him to bark at her.

He remained silent. He lifted his head. He looked exhausted, his eyes bloodshot.

She was trying to grasp the significance of what was happening. His day's growth of stubble shadowed his cheeks making him look piratical and dangerous. And she knew what she felt physically for him wasn't ever going to go away. She'd already tried to banish those feelings without success. Where had he gone? She hated that about him, he'd never given her any explanations. Withholding part of himself. Something clenched in her chest. She felt close to him, yet so far away. Her stomach soured. The forlorn expression on his face made her want to cry and gather him close to her chest and soothe him. But she was afraid. Earlier he had frozen her out. The bitter cold had surrounded her heart. Santo's face looked as if it had been cast in stone. She waited for him to speak.

"Why aren't you sleeping?" he said, his voice gravelly and gruff.

She glanced at him and shrugged. She pretended nonchalance. "Restless, I guess. I came to get some water. You? How long have you been sitting here in the dark?"

"Not long," he said, his tone cold and hard. Abrupt.

She found a bottle of water and offered him one. He shook his head, so she put it back.

The wind was picking up outside, and it sounded like a storm was brewing. Maddie sipped from the plastic bottle, the water soothing her parched throat.

"Is it going to storm?" she inquired.

"Sounds like it," he said. "It's in the fore-
cast."

Menial conversation. He seemed so distance,
detached. So, unlike him. He was always direct and
precise. She never known him not to be self-assured
and shrewd in business and pleasure. But now he
looked dejected and unsure of himself.

His distinct features were grim. Chiseled in
stone.

Maddie trudged ahead. "Did you take care of
your pressing matters?" she boldly asked.

He froze her with his look. "Don't," his voice
ground out, hard and unforgiving. "My evening has
been less than ideal." His accent was heavier than
normal.

She moved forward, sitting her water down.
He clasped her wrist. The pressure tight.

She looked down at his fingers wrapped
around her wrist, then up into his blustery eyes.
They were brewing like the storm sweeping in outside.

"When you left," his voice was strained and
rough, "I went on a drinking binge."

Swallowing, she raised her free hand and
cupped his cheek, surprise lit her eyes. Guilt
clutched at her. Sorrow filled her eyes. What could
she say or do to take the sorrow from his face? What

could she do to fix this?

"You never drink," she said simply.

"No, I don't, but your departure sent me over the edge. The alcohol numbed the pain." He pulled her between his parted thighs and placed his hands around her waist.

Maddie tensed beneath his touch, but only briefly.

"What are you saying?" she whispered, strain in her voice.

"I'm saying, that when you left, I was tortured, I felt betrayed." Instead of the cool, controlled, man he was, his body language, his voice, indicated a pain so profound that it was imbedded deep.

She put her hands upon his shoulders, and he leaned his forehead onto her chest. Her heart pounded, skipping a momentary beat. She'd never seen this side of Santo, needy, seeking her comfort and compassion. She placed her fingers in his hair. She massaged his scalp.

"Why didn't you tell me?" Maddie asked, her expression scrutinizing.

He raised his head; his face grew guarded. "I tried. You wouldn't listen. I had no control over your decisions."

"You didn't come after me," she cried. "I waited, you know, for your call, something, but there was nothing. Absolutely nothing."

"I know," he said matter-of-factly. "The timing was all wrong, our marriage was all wrong."

She huffed with grief. She twisted from his grip. As quick as she weakened she regained strength. "You're right," she said defensively, hurt shrouding her chest. "The timing is still wrong."

"Maddie, why did you go without giving me a chance?"

"I thought it was what you wanted. I thought," her voice wobbled, "with me gone you could bring Vanessa back into your life." Her eyes captured and held his, waiting for his answer. "Why didn't you?"

He paced the room, then turned. "I didn't want Vanessa, ever. I told you it was a mistake. All of it. She planted herself in my bed. I was as shocked as you to find her there." He saw that old thread of jealously rearing its ugly head. "Listen to me, bella, Vanessa is a conniving manipulator. She used me for her own personal gain."

Angrily, Maddie shook her head. "Who cares if you want Vanessa, Santo, but don't deny the child. The child is blameless." His soft-spoken words failed to convince her he was innocent.

"Accidenti! Matteo isn't my child. I have DNA results to prove it. The child belongs to Marco.

Vanessa lied. You see, Marco married Vanessa. He is miserably in love with her."

Maddie froze. Her eyes narrowed as he caught and held her gaze. Disbelief filled her eyes. "What do you mean? When? Why didn't you tell me?"

It felt as if the sheets of rain, pouring outside, were pelting her skin. The sting was unbearable. She was having trouble comprehending everything he'd said.

"I was a fool to not notify you. A couple of months after you were gone, Marco came to me. Pleading for my help. The guilt was tearing him up. He'd fallen for Vanessa a long time ago. The child is his, tesoro."

Maddie shook her head. Disbelief written upon her face. "Why tell me this now?" she asked shakily.

He clasped each of her biceps. His grip was firm. He stared deep into her troubled eyes, pleading for her to understand. "It's time to clear the air. We owe it to ourselves. Start fresh." He shook his head. "I stepped in the apartment in the city tonight and thought what an idiot I've been. Although Marco was highly inebriated tonight he was brutally honest. We need to stop this, Maddie. Start fresh." He raked his hand through his hair. "Tomorrow I'm putting the apartment on the market. Something I should've done a long time ago. Nothing there but bad memories."

She moved away from him. Her guarded heart afraid to believe him. Trust him.

"I don't believe you. If that were the truth then why keep it from me? Why let me suffer all those months, years, believing a lie?" Her lip began to tremble. She bit it and fought back the tears. She wasn't a prone to tears, but here she was about to shed them again for him. "I sacrificed my career, my family, my life for you. And now you tell me this." He desperately wanted her to accept the truth.

"I made sacrifices too. Didn't I give you a good life? Everything you could possibly want or need?"

She bowed her head, her hair sheltering her face. "Everything," she whispered, "but the one thing I wanted the most, your love."

He stepped back, she knew it was too late. She felt his withdrawal.

He wanted to shake her and make her understand. This wasn't easy for him. Not at all. He was trying so hard to give her what she wanted, but love.

Love was nothing but a word. It didn't mean that he couldn't give her what she needed. Commitment didn't need love to be stable and enduring.

Their physical connection was hot, hot, hot. Wasn't that enough? Look at Marco, fallen in love with Vanessa, and it was nothing but disaster. The two of them continued to torture and hurt each other. He would be faithful. Wasn't that enough? Marriage required commitment. He gave that. He didn't understand her continued resistance. Emotion was overrated. They didn't need it.

Maddie tried to remain calm. Santo's facial imagery sent her heart plummeting. When she mentioned love he back stepped. Her pulse jump started in her chest. Their lovemaking was a testimony that she still wanted him. That burning need had not subsided. But did she love him? She didn't think so. She'd buried her love, along with her vulnerability, a long time ago.

She was a stronger woman for it.

She was torn between wanting him, needing him, or walking away. Her instincts told her to take the fight or flight stance. And right now, flight seemed the logical choice. She needed time to think. Collect her thoughts. To decipher all that he'd said.

His eyes were haunted. Sad.

It nearly broke her heart to see him this way.

"No matter what you think of me, Maddie. No matter where you go. Believe me when I say that I'm telling you the truth. I never cheated on you then, nor will I now."

Torrents of rain pelted the glass. The raging storm didn't compare to her violent emotions. She saw the truth written in his steely eyes. Santo was a man of honor. Integrity was important to him. His privacy was kept at all costs. She now knew her jealous rage had drove her to believe the worst. She couldn't take it back or change the past.

"I'm so sorry, Santo." Her eyelids closed shielding her expressive eyes. Then she darted a glance in his direction. His eyes burned. She struggled to get air into her burning lungs. He was too much to resist.

Desire crashed upon him. His body tensed. His fists clenched at his sides. The ever-present emotion lay bubbling just beneath the surface. Consuming him. The old saying "the truth shall set you free" was true. He felt as if the load bearing burdens, he'd carried for so long, had lifted. His lip twitched. Blood pulsed through his veins.

At that moment she looked so delicate. So, captivating. He wanted her with everything in him. Her ratty T-shirt covered everything, but so little. Her pert little breasts were outlined beneath the material.

He groaned, she threw him a startled look. Her eyes widened in acknowledgement.

His intent was clear. He wanted her.

She licked her dry lips. Her nipples pebbled into rock hard buds. She'd always heard that make-up sex was the best. The moment his hand touched her satiny smooth flesh, they were lost.

The pounding rain on the rooftop only intensified the urgency. Santo clasped her protruding breast before ravaging her mouth with his. He picked her up and strode though the house to his bedroom.

She clasped her arms tightly around his neck. Hanging on to the hope that he would let his guard down.

The bedroom was as Maddie remembered. Masculine shades of gray with hints of black. The massive bed was the same. He gently laid her down. She was entranced. She watched him shed his jacket, his shirt and his pants followed. The T-shirt she was wearing had ridden up on her thighs. He made her run from hot to cold. She hated how he made her feel but rejoiced in it at the same time. He was a wicked devil. So, hypnotizing. So easily he could destroy her resistance.

His eyes gleamed with arousal. He came to her. His body covering her pliable form. She moaned her pleasure. Her toes curled. She tugged on his hair. No matter the barriers, no matter her hesitation, the outcome was the same. Unquenchable desire.

Knowing he'd been faithful to her was a powerful aphrodisiac. She pulled his mouth to hers and took control. She darted her tongue inside and erotically danced with his. His arousal was evident. His erection rock hard against her thigh.

He rose, putting space between them, and tugged the shirt from her trembling body. He probed her straining breasts. Their fullness filling his hands. Her fingers clasped the duvet cover, and her knees splayed apart granting him entry. Rational thinking left her. She could feel nothing but heated sensation driving her. The invisible string of heightened awareness wove its way straight to her core.

He gave a little groan of sensual promise when his fingers found her heated center. She was moist, hot, and ready. He clenched his teeth, restraining the need to seek immediate release. How could he want her so much after being so deeply satisfied before?

He teased her whispering sweet Italian endearments on her skin between kisses.

"I want you," he ground out unsteadily.

She tossed her head from side to side teetering on climax. His tongue laved her nipples, and his roaming fingers wondered relentlessly over her skin.

His machinations so clever and precise. She tried to retain control. She truly did, but he was the master. Her breathing became pants. Her heels dug into the bed, and her calf muscles tensed from the strain. She was on the brink. He was bringing her closer and closer to orgasm. She tried to hold off.

And then he was there his tip at her entrance. Teasing her, making her scream. His first full thrust filled her completely.

"Take me, Santo. Now," she cried.

He thrust inside her again and again. She clamped her thighs around him taking him deeper and deeper. He held on tight, gritting his teeth until he felt her give way around him, then he exploded. In that moment, that second, she had a powerful hold over him. He would have promised her anything.

She was the only woman that made him lose that kind of control during lovemaking. With others he'd always remained detached. No feelings, robotically functioning. With Maddie, he momentarily lost his head. He was staking his claim. But had he claimed her, or her him? At this point he didn't know. Their chemical combustion was potent. A dangerous drug.

He kissed her. Licked her trembling lips. He could taste the faint trace of his aftershave upon her mouth. He couldn't imagine letting her go again. He had branded her for him. Only him.

"Thank you," she whispered against his cheek. "Thank you for being honest. Thank you for wanting me."

Her simple words stabbed his heart. Wasn't that what he wanted? Her complete acceptance. Her dreamlike expression caused him guilt. He could offer his body, but could he offer her his heart. There was a fine line between logical and irrational.

He rolled away. She opened her eyes. She knew the moment he was distancing himself. She missed his heat already.

She felt exposed. Her heart on her chest. A fraud. She didn't know where they were going. How much longer could they give each so much pleasure, yet so much pain? Hell, on earth.

It felt like he was trying to steal her heart away. Capture it and take away her defense and then toss it back.

"Maddie." He brushed her shoulder.

She turned her back to him pulling the blankets over her. "Goodnight, Santo. I'm tired."

He didn't say anything, but he rose from the bed, donned his pants, then left the room.

She cuddled into a ball misery filling her. Why did it always end this way? She looked out the darkened window, rain ran in rivulets down the glass, and tears flowed like the rain down her cheeks. Sobs racked her body moisture dampening the pillow.

Santo still hadn't made any promises.

. . .

Darkness shrouded Santo as he made his way barefoot and shirtless into the study. Lightning bolts streaked through the sky matching his turbulent thoughts. He stood in front of the window and watched the drenching downpour.

He'd taken Marco's crazy advice and poured his heart out to his irritant wife. What good had it done? They ended up right back where they had started, in bed. Not that he was complaining. He liked it there, he wanted her there.

But he didn't like that she made him lose his mind. The old ideology of mind-blowing sex was absolutely true when it came to Maddie.

She was heart-wrenching beautiful. She met him kiss for kiss, stroke for stroke. His body tightened in remembrance. The thought of her lying beneath another man, saying she loved him, becoming his wife, was unthinkable. His gut clenched tightly. He'd be damned if he'd allow that to happen.

She was his.

Since the first moment he'd met her, she'd been branded his.

And now that she was back in his bed he had an unbearable craving for her touch. She caused his blood to race and sizzle through his veins from the simplest touch. He rubbed his hand across the back of his neck. He should feel relaxed after sex, but every muscle in his body was rigid and taut. He had too many thoughts swirling around in his head. Mixed emotions. He felt restless.
He could use a stiff drink to calm him but that wasn't the answer.   What was the answer?

And now he had his grandmother's stipulations to contend with. For a brief moment he imagined Maddie pregnant with his child. The seed he'd plant growing inside her. He shook his head. Would she want that, his child? He didn't know. He didn't know what she wanted anymore. There was a time when he thought he did, but had he been mistaken. They were hot and cold, a raging storm, with impossible odds.

His jaw locked, his lips compressed in a flat line, his smoky grey gaze troubled. His heart rate thundered against his rib-cage. He was furious with Maddie for making him feel this way. Unsure of himself and his decisions. He exercised exactly standards in all his transactions, but his marriage transaction was causing him to be jumbled up into knots. His subtle negotiations hadn't worked.

He wanted to storm to the bedroom and demand she give him answers. Demand that she never leaves. Demand that she told him what he wanted to hear.

But he couldn't. It would have the opposite affect and make her run.

Could he be content with a loveless marriage, full of passion?

He thought after she'd run the first time he'd formed an immunity to her but he hadn't. Why did it still sting so much? It was pressing down upon him like a vise.

His jaw ticked.

He had told her about his faithfulness. Had that been a mistake? Would she play it against him?

Tomorrow he was flying to London. He had some crucial negotiations that demanded his undivided attention. Staying focused was key to business success. His mind couldn't be thinking about a woman lying in his home, in his bed. He had to be single-minded. He was a lethal businessman and gave his undivided attention to every detail of a business strategy. Maddie was a serious diversion. One he couldn't afford right now.

He needed her with him. He must reclaim his

wayward wife. Their chemistry was valuable ammunition. She couldn't resist his touch. Nor, he hers,
if he was being honest with himself.

The buzzing in his head intensified. He had
the makings of a powerful headache.   Massaging his
temples, his eyes squinted in the rain-soaked darkness. His decision made; he strode from the room.

At the door of the bedroom, he paused. What
if she refused? How would he convince her to come
to London with him? A methodical seduction was his
best devised plan.

He opened the door.

She lay curled on the edge of the bed. Her
wild curls splayed upon his pillow. His heart skipped
a beat. Inexplicable thoughts spiraled through him,
unidentifiable thoughts, for which he had no logical
explanation.

His wife had imbedded herself beneath his
skin. He shed his pants, climbed under the Egyptian
cotton sheets, and began to seduce his wife all over
again.

Chapter 9

The limousine was waiting the moment they stepped off his private jet. London was overcast and dreary and goosebumps formed on Maddie's arms. She viewed Santo from beneath her thick lashes. His wide, sensual mouth was smiling as he shook hands with the appointed chauffeur. They engaged in a polite exchange of words before Santo opened the door ushering her inside.

Santo stood tall while he waited for her to climb in. His towering height, athletic body, and stunning good looks demanded attention. Her, along with every other female in the vicinity, appreciated him. When God was passing out fabulous looks, Santo was first in line. He was flawless. His perfect olive complexion, mesmerizing grey eyes, and beautiful white teeth were a perfect combination.

He climbed in and spread his long legs out in front of him. She smelled a faint whiff of his aftershave causing her to blush. She'd been wearing that same scent upon her skin from their lovemaking.

The floodgates opened and unwilling memories from last night rolled through her mind. She had run her fingers through his thick, glossy, black hair, fisting the soft strands as he'd ravaged her soft skin over and over again. They'd had very little sleep, and the dark shadow beneath her eyes reflected it.

He, on the other hand, looked fresh, collected and ready to face the world. She'd let down her guard, no, her guard had been demolished after his expert hands had brought her to release too many times to count.

The corners of his mouth curled into a semblance of a smile. She was certain he knew what she was thinking. He placed his hand upon her bare, exposed knee causing ripples of awareness to spiral along her spine.

The briefest touch could set her soul on fire.

Removing his hand, he whispered. "Later."

She didn't respond. What did you say to that? His audacity was domineering. He could read her mind so easily. He knew she was thinking about their bedroom encounters. Redness crept into her cheeks. No matter how many times they were intimate, he still had the ability to make her blush. She remained acutely aware of him. Her nerve endings stayed taxed and alert. Unsettled emotions whirled through her when she was in his presence.

He scrutinized her briefly, but she couldn't read his thoughts. His eyes remained blank.

Opening his brief case, he shuffled through several papers, while Maddie turned her attention to the passing scenery.

They were falling right back into old patterns. The explosives in the bedroom. Her career being put on hold while she followed him around the world to further his.

She loved his drive and stamina. His commitment to his company. She wouldn't ask him to change it but wanted to continue hers. Honestly, he'd never ask her to give up her job, it was understood.

She turned to look at him when he spoke. "We're attending a small cocktail party after we freshen up. My clients want me to meet them for dinner and drinks." He caught her glance, waiting for her reaction.

"Okay," she said. "I'm not sure I brought anything to wear that's appropriate."

"It's taken care of," he replied.

Of course, it was, she thought. Santo was always one step ahead of any situation. If only circumstances were different.

They reached the hotel. The door to the limo was whisked open. She stuck out her hand and was helped from the car. Santo was given the royal treatment, which he was accustomed to. Everything had been arranged before his arrival. The elevator whisked them to the top floor and the penthouse suite.

Only the best for Santo Barrella.

He placed his hand on the small of her back as they exited through the sliding doors. Placing his brief case on the floor he swiped the key card to let them in.

The room was fantastic as Maddie knew it would be. A bank of windows overlooked the Thames River. She stepped out onto the balcony and encountered all the dazzling lights of the city.

Santo stepped outside and stood beside her. "This view is amazing, isn't it?"

She nodded not finding the words to describe it.

She tilted her head to look up into his dazzling face. "Is this where you always stay?" she asked. "I don't remember it."

"Yes, my last visits to London have been here. It serves my purpose."

She laughed softly. "I'm sure it does."

She turned and went back inside. The dining room walls were surrounded with mirrored glass reflecting all the sparkling crystal on the table. A fire crackled in the fireplace and through double doors was a fully equipped office outfitted with triple screens for conference calls.

A winding staircase led to the upper level with black onyx steps and gleaming silver balustrade.

"Shall we?" he asked, following her up the steps.

The bedroom was huge with an adjoining tiled bathroom and walk in closet. Upon the bed were several clothing bags with designer labels.

Santo pointed at them. "I didn't know what you would need, or like, so I had several choices delivered. I'll use the other bathroom so you can take your time." He quickly gave her a peck on the lips and left the room.

She stood stock still and looked around feeling uncomfortable for the first time. It had been so long since she had attended these things with him she'd forgotten how to act. Really, she'd never known how to act. She'd always stood on the sidelines, in the shadows, attempting to stay out of the limelight. And before, Santo had always accepted her vying to be inconspicuous. First, she stripped out of her clothes and got into the shower. The rain shower fixture cascaded water onto her aching shoulders. She stood several minutes letting the spray relax her muscles.

She felt, eyes closed, until she found the heated, plush towel and wrapped it turban style around her head. Finding another she wrapped it around her wet, slick body.

Santo hadn't missed a thing when providing the necessities for her. She found the lingerie, shoes, and jewelry to go with the clothing.

Opening the bags, she viewed the array of sophisticated dresses. The colorful hues of blue, red, black, and various other colors were spread out on the bed.

She chose a simple design in a shade of royal blue. The sequined halter top graced her neck and more sequins trailed underneath the arms and around the back. Sweeping her hair on top of her head she pinned it in various loops and twists. She left a few wisps hanging on the sides and back. She chose some strappy sandals that matched the sequins on the dress. She placed a diamond bracelet around her wrist to complete the ensemble.

She looked in the full-length mirror and touched up the shadows beneath her eyes with make-up. Placing some pink upon her lips she turned when hearing Santo enter the room.

He gave her the once over and nodded his approval. His piercing gaze captured hers. His steely gaze darkened with appreciation.

"Is this okay?" She twirled around, and her own widened eyes encompassed his dark, charcoal gray tux. He looked unbelievably handsome.

"More than okay," he stated, he held out his hand.

She took it and smiled sweetly.

His smart phone buzzed. Pulling it from his jacket pocket he glanced at the screen and then frowned.

"Who is it?" she asked.

"It's not important. I'll take care of it later. Are you ready?"

Maddie nodded. He was still keeping secrets. A twinge of jealously began eating at her, but she heaved in a deep breath and followed him out the door.

The car whisked them to a five-star restaurant and bar. The maître d led them to a table surrounded with a group of business men. A couple of women were seated too, they threw Santo sly, appreciative glances.

Santo gave Maddie that look.

She forced her emotions behind a blank mask pasting a smile on her face. He pulled her out a chair then sat beside her. He rubbed his knee against hers beneath the table. Her eyes widened briefly, and she gazed at his profile, but he didn't blink.

The waiter came to take their orders as Santo exchanged pleasantries with the group of men. Maddie listened intently for a while then phased out the conversation that meant nothing to her. The intricacies of computer software didn't interest her.

One of the women engaged Santo in conversation several times. Her smile was all pretense, no substance. Maddie placed her hand on Santo's forearm staking her claim. He gave her a dazzling smile warming her blood. The woman looked at her hand then gave her a nasty, haughty look. Maddie smiled her satisfaction. There was power in having the man other women wanted.

They finished their meal. A band started up in the other room. One man, named Akinari Horita, insisted they join them. The bar was dim, and the dance floor was less than crowded. Mr. Horita, a short Japanese man with distinguished gray at his temples, bowed before asking her to dance. She knew it would be rude to refuse so she accepted.

The blond goddess who'd been hitting on Santo all night leaped at the opportunity to drag him onto the floor.

Maddie was having a hard time focusing on Mr. Horita's question when her eyes stayed glued to Santo.

He cleared his throat. Maddie smiled politely and gave him her undivided attention.

"It's refreshing to see a woman so in love with her husband," he said with clear, concise English. "Santo is a wonderful person and a fierce business opponent."

Maddie lowered her lashes, blushing prettily. "Yes," she said softly.

He was mistaken. She didn't love Santo, did she? Absolutely impossible.

Mr. Horita gently squeezed her hand. "No need to be embarrassed. I can see he feels the same about you. I think his mind has wondered from business many times," he laughed, "and that isn't like my powerful friend at all. "You're blessed."

Maddie wanted to deny his words but didn't.

"Do you have a family?" she asked instead.

He smiled and nodded. "Yes, I've been with my wife for forty years, and we have three grown children. My wife and I are blessed with two wonderful grandchildren, which we spoil terribly. Have you and Santo thought about children?" He whirled her around the smooth floor, Maddie had to look down to see his smiling eyes.

"We've discussed it," she blushed again.

"Such beautiful children you will make," he said.

It was then that Santo tapped his shoulder. "May I?" he asked.

Mr. Horita nodded and stepped away.

"Your wife is a special woman, Santo. Treasure her always," Mr. Horita told him.

He nodded his agreement.

Santo pulled her into his arms bringing her close. Air escaped her lungs in one big whoosh when his hands splayed across her exposed skin.

"Mr. Horita seemed to have a lot to talk about," he said, his eyes holding hers.

Maddie nodded. "He was telling me about his family." She licked her lips when he continued to hold her glance.

"Yes, family is very important to him." Her heartbeat sped up as he glided her smoothly and expertly around the dance floor. "Is business good?" she asked.

"Yes," he nodded. "We'll talk more tomorrow, but everything I've negotiated will be done."

The song ended, Santo led her off the floor. "We'll just say our goodnights," he said. "I'm ready to get back and relax."

She mumbled her goodnights after him as he escorted her out the door. London's skyline was shimmering with all the night lights giving it an ethereal glow. The car was waiting to take them back. He picked up the bottom of her dress and tucked it in around her. His fingers brushed against her smooth calf, and when he rose smoke filled his eyes.

She bit the corner of her lip, and she knew he was instantly turned on. She did it purposefully.

The drive to the penthouse was accomplished

within minutes. Santo marched her through the lobby to the bank of elevators taking them to the top floor.

As soon as they entered the suite, he kicked the door shut with his foot, his lips were on hers. She moaned her pleasure.

"I've been waiting all night for this," he said.

"Me too," she blatantly admitted.

And that was all the encouragement he needed. His fingers expertly unhooked the halter and unzipped the rest. It fell in a puddle upon the floor. He stepped back and looked at her clothed only in the lacy underthings. His eyes glinted their pleasure.

"You're beautiful," he groaned his pleasure.

She stepped from within the circle of cloth her sandals clicking against the marble floor. She shivered not from cold but pleasure.

And then his hands were upon her laying claim to the exposed flesh. She swayed toward him, and he caught her in his arms. His shaking hands plied at his tie and tossed it to the side. Her fingers slipped the row of buttons from the holes opening his crisp white shirt. The hair on his chest tickled her fingertips. He pressed his forehead against hers breathing deeply.

"Mio caro, I can't get enough of you."
He pulled her impatiently up the stairs to the bed-

room. This was why he brought her. This was why he couldn't leave her behind. He craved her body and her touch.

He shrugged his broad shoulders from his jacket and shirt then cast them onto the floor. His bare chest gleamed in the firelight. Maddie could feel heat building at her center. She touched his cheek. He clasped her hand and sucked on each fingertip. She sighed with yearning.

He laid her hand upon his chest while he went to her breasts. He lifted their weight nearly popping the nipples from the restraints of her bra. Her fingernails dug into his flesh causing him to flinch.

He released the clasp on her bra and tossed it onto the bed. Lowering his head his mouth clamped upon her luscious pink areola sucking hard. The pressure sent shooting shards of desire crashing through her.

"Santo," she moaned. "Oh, Santo."

"Tell me what you want, amore mio," he said laving both puckered nipples.

"I want...I want," she couldn't form a thought. She could only focus on the pleasure of his lips.

He laughed. Picking her up he gently put her on the bed. "I want to be inside you my sexy, little siren," he said unbuttoning his pants.

He climbed onto the bed. His perfect nude body silhouetted from the backdrop of the glowing fire. He plied her legs apart exposing the secrets between her legs. His mouth ran a trail of kisses along the inside of her thighs. She pulled on his hair. Then his tongue found what it had been searching for. He kissed the very moist center of her. She nearly screamed with joy. He kissed, he sucked and massaged until she came apart. Her release sending her skyrocketing out of control.

When she stilled he slid onto her moist body and found her lips. She could taste the essence of her wicked desire on his lips.

She clamped his taunt buttocks. Squeezing their firmness. His splendid erection pressed against her thighs searching, seeking entrance. She shifted her hips and the tip found her red-hot center.

He entered her, driving, sliding in and out as her climax began to build. She cried his name over and over. Urging him to move faster and faster until they exploded together.

They lay spent. Their breathing labored.

"Thank you," he whispered softly against her cheek.

She turned and captured his lips and kissed him deeply then said. "No, thank you. The pleasure was all mine."

They turned down the covers and lay spent in each other's arms finding comfort. Maddie put her head on his shoulder and soon fell asleep.

Santo watched her so relaxed and content. Tenderness filled his chest. He couldn't imagine life without her again. She'd captured his heart once, could she do it again.

That was his last thought as his eyes grew heavy, and he too found sleep.

. . .

When Maddie awoke Santo was gone. She didn't hear any signs of him in the bathroom. Rolling over she scrambled from the bed and into the shower.

Recollections of last night raced through her thoughts making her shiver. She could search the rest of her life and never find a better lover than Santo Barrella.

Satisfying a woman came naturally to him, and he delivered every time. She smiled while languishing in the pounding water jets.

Dressing she made her way downstairs. She could smell food and found a loaded tray. Pouring some coffee, she sipped it and looked around the room, but Santo was gone. She assumed his business meetings had demanded his attention.

Wrapping her fingers around the coffee mug she made her way outside onto the balcony and looked down at the bustling city. Everyone had somewhere to go but her. She felt extremely alone.

Pulling her phone from her pocket she called home. After a couple rings her mom answered.

"Maddie," she said excited. "How are you? We've been worried sick about you. Why haven't called?"

Maddie smiled it felt so good to hear her mom's voice. "I'm fine," she reassured her. "I'm in London. Santo has business."

"How is Santo?" her mom asked.

"He's great," Maddie told her.

Her dad cut in. "Is he treating you okay? No problems?"

"Everything is fine, I promise," she said. "We are trying to work some things out. I'll be back home before you know it."

"You're not staying?" she could hear the disappointment in her mom's voice.

"No, mom. It's complicated." Maddie felt the tight clinch of regret twisting inside her.

"We had hoped," her mom started, but Maddie stopped her.

"I know, but we don't always get what we

want," Maddie turned and found Santo looking at her, fury in his eyes. Maddie gasped.

"Listen mom. I've got to go. We'll talk later," and she hung up.

"Santo," she said.

Tension filled the air between them. How much had he heard? All of it.

"I thought we worked out the details," Santo growled tightly. "Why tell your family you're heading home?"

"Why not?" Maddie tossed back. I am."

"After this," he pointed toward the bedroom.

She frowned. "What?" she asked. "So, we had great sex that doesn't solve anything. We are as far from reconciliation as when we first begun."
He forced himself to remain calm by breathing in deeply. He watched her slender frame tense with rebellion. Her cat-like hazel eyes narrowed and were combative. He strode forward shortening the distance between them.

She stood straighter preparing for battle.

"I thought we cleared up all the misconceived notions of why you left. I explained about Vanessa and the lies," his eyes narrowed in annoyance. His deep voice was curt and businesslike.

How could he do that Maddie wondered? Turn off his feelings. Become so cold and concise. Treat her like a number on a spreadsheet.

"I know," she said sitting down her mug. "I get it about Vanessa. But what about me?" she threw back spitefully. "You still treat me like a play-thing. When you get tired of me, what then?" she asked. "Discard me? Send me home? What?" she asked furiously.

His eyes narrowed into slits. "That's ridic-ulous. I've never treated you like a possession or a plaything. I respect that you're my wife."

"Do you?" She wanted to stomp her foot. She was churning inside. She couldn't even explain why she was so mad at him. She didn't even know her-self. All the pent-up emotions she'd carried for so many years were flying to the surface.

"Dio," he raked his fingers through his hair. "This conversation is pointless. You're spouting absolutely ridiculous accusations that aren't true. Stop it," he said clasping her upper arms holding her still when she tried to jerk away. "I brought you here with me, didn't I? If I wanted you gone I would have said so. We can't ignore what we have between us, Maddie. It's inevitable that we pursue it to the end."

She tossed her head from side to side trying to banish the awareness shooting through her. "I want closure, Santo. I want to go home and drown in my own sorrow. Find happiness."

"Happiness with who, Edward? Can't we have that, Maddie?" It felt like a knotted fist sucker-punched him in the solar plexus. How could he please her? Helplessness filled him. He didn't know what she wanted.

She pulled back. He let her go. She turned away and looked, through tear filled eyes, at the river below.

Santo watched her shoulders tightened and tense. Frustration and extreme irritation filled him. He didn't touch her but stepped alongside of her. He tentatively touched her hand, and when she didn't pull away, he wove his fingers through hers. He wanted her so much. His body throbbed for her. He turned her toward him, cupping her cheek. Moisture wetted his hand. "I want you, mio caro. I always have."

She looked at him. His grey eyes softened to velvet. She sniffled. He handed her his handkerchief. Blowing her nose, she looked up into his questioning eyes. "And I want you, Santo. But physical attraction just isn't enough."

"I know," he said. "But that's all I've got to give right now."

"I realize that." She lowered her head sadness filling her eyes.

"My business is done here," he said. "I

thought we'd tour the city, but if you want to fly home we will."

"I want to fly home," she told him. Her stomach clenched. It was his home not hers.

He nodded. "Then pack your things. I'll make the arrangements."

He walked away pulling his phone from his pocket.

She'd hurt him. She couldn't help herself. Inside he was still on the phone. Maddie went up and packed the things she'd brought leaving the rest lying on the bed. He eyed the designer bags, didn't say a thing, then got his own.

The transition from the hotel to the car then the plane went smoothly. Not a word was spoken. Santo conducted several business calls completely ignoring her. She felt terrible. She'd gone from sleeping beside him to complete misery. Sometimes shutting off your feelings was better. Then the hurt would subside or never be part of the equation.

A shiver ran along her spine, and she wondered how the heck she was going to get through all of this.

Chapter 10

She was giving him the cold shoulder.
Since they'd returned from London, she hadn't spoken to him. Nor had she slept with him. She'd avoided him.

The days had passed slowly.

She missed his touch, his lips, but refused to dwell on it.

Some mornings she had heard him become brisk and short with Isabella. Maddie was restless. Santo left her alone for the most part. He joined her for a few meals, but other than that they were both moody and unapproachable.

But this morning when she stepped out onto the terrace, he was there. He looked fabulous as always, and she looked at him longingly.

He'd read her thoughts. She could see it in his eyes. His charcoal grey orbs darkened immediately. He still wanted her, she was sure.

"Good morning," he said taking a seat at the table.

"Morning," she mumbled.

He eyed her white denim shorts, tank top, and bare feet. Her hair was pulled up into a ponytail, her face free of cosmetics.

She looked so fresh and innocent. Almost like a school girl.

"Are you hungry?" he asked.

"A little," she admitted. Her stomach had been feeling a little bit off lately. Almost queasy. She poured a glass of the fresh squeezed orange juice sipping it gingerly.

She knew he'd been gone a lot, but he looked tired. He poured himself a cup of coffee then filled his plate.

"I'm flying out tomorrow. I'd like for you to come with me."

Her heart lurched. Their last trip had been a disaster. "Why?" she mouthed surprised.

His lips compressed. "Why would you ask? I want you fully and completely ensconced in my life. I want the world to know you are my wife," he paused, "and my bedpartner. I don't want any doubt about the role you play in my life."

Her stomach did a little flip. She licked her suddenly dry lips. "So, now I'm your wife?" She gave him a surprised, annoyed glance.

"Yes, and you will be by my side." It wasn't a request but an order.

If there was one thing Maddie disliked it was to be ordered around. "I will not bow down to your demands. If I go," her eyes bore into his, "it will be because I choose to."

"Si, naturalmente. I want you to decide for yourself. You have until morning. We fly out tomorrow for New York."

"What?" She threw him an excited look. "You're flying to New York? I'll be packed and ready."

His heart lurched when he saw the excitement light her face. But he refused to show it. "I thought you'd change your mind."

. . .

Shortly after take-off Maddie settled into the plush leather seat on the plane. No matter how many times she'd flown on his private jet it took some getting used to. They were served a light lunch on expensive, fragile china.

Santo sat next to her but was occupied by figures on his computer screen. She picked up a magazine and perused the pages not really paying attention to the words.

The phone lying beside him began to ring. Maddie looked down at the screen. Her gut twisted savagely. It was Vanessa. Her hauntingly beautiful image stared back at her.

Santo picked it up and slid the bar to answer. She couldn't catch the conversation because he spoke in rapid Italian. He wasn't pleased, nor was Maddie. He ended the call, and she waited for him to say something but he didn't. He looked back down at the computer.

When she thought she could trust him he did this? She crossed her legs then she uncrossed them. Crossed them again. She put the magazine down and stared out the window.

"Go ahead Maddie. Say what's on your mind," he told her.

She looked across at him, his eyebrow lifted mockingly. She bit her lip in aggravation. "What do you want me to say?" Maddie's eyes burned holes into his chest.

He smirked. "Whatever that little suspicious mind of yours has conjured up."

"Why wouldn't I be suspicious?" she huffed her bottom lip jutting out in a pout. "Vanessa is my, our nemesis."

"You have nothing to worry about. Marco's out again, and she wanted me to bring him home." He clasped her wrist. "I told her I was gone. Simple as that."

Maddie nodded. "Fine. Whatever." She looked down at this hand on her arm. "It doesn't matter to me."

"Liar," he laughed.

She snorted and pulled away from his touch. "Think what you like. I'm tired. I need a nap."

He pointed to the back. "Go lie down. I'll wake you when we land."

She stood and passed by him and made her way to the back of the plane. The bedroom was fully equipped and comfortable. Lying down she fell fast asleep.

She woke when the plane braked on the tarmac. Rubbing her eyes, she sat up and gulped when the room began to spin around. She clutched her stomach and felt nauseous.

Santo stood at the door and saw her ashen features. "Maddie," he inquired rushing to her side. "Are you okay? Here," he said bracing her back, "sit still."

Sweat broke out upon her brow, and she gulped in several puffs of air. Sitting perfectly still she waited for the sensation to pass.

"Can you lie back down?" he asked worriedly. "Let me help you." She nodded because she couldn't speak. Plumping up the pillows he eased her back. Maddie sighed in relief. "Be still," he said standing up and heading to the bathroom.

He came back with a cool, wet washcloth and placed it on her forehead.

"Thanks," she whispered the dizziness finally subsiding.

"Are you alright? Should I get a doctor?" He placed his hand against her cheek checking her temperature.

"I'm fine. It must've been something I ate,"

she smiled. "I feel better already."

"You're sure?" he said. "No sense in taking any chances," he said. "You lie still, and I'll get everything ready. Can you make it to the car?" He asked, concern in his eyes.

"Yes," she promised. "I felt a little dizzy for a moment, but it's better now."
He hesitated a bit then nodded. "I'll be back. Don't you dare move," he ordered before walking out the door.

She truly felt better. She didn't know what happened. Maybe she'd sat up too fast or, like she'd said, something she ate. Generally, Maddie was pretty healthy. She never caught the flu bug. Gingerly she sat up and placed her feet on the floor testing the waters. Nothing. Her stomach remained calm. Whew, she thought. The last thing she needed was to be sick.

"I told you to stay put," Santo said when he got back to the room.

She smiled prettily. "I know, but I'm fine. I feel completely fine."

He shook his head about to say something else, but then, changed his mind. "Come on. The car's waiting."

He placed his hand at the small of her back and stuck close behind her. Thank goodness the sickness had passed.

Exiting the plane, a blast of cold, New York air stung her face. She wrapped her coat tighter against her to block the wind.

"Dio," Santo exclaimed, "I forgot how cold New York can be."

He rushed her to the waiting car, freezing snow blanketed the ground. She looked up to meet his hooded, glinting eyes. He smiled despite the cold. A vision of their mingled breath circled in the frigid air.

Maddie smiled her thanks when he tucked her into the cozy warmth of the heated limo. Santo tapped on the closed partition to instruct the driver of her apartment address.

She cast him a surprised glance. "You're dropping me off at my apartment," she asked, relief shone in her eyes.

He nodded. "Yes, but I'm staying too."

"That isn't necessary. You won't be comfort-able," she assured him. "It's small and cramped." He turned his knees brushing hers. "I'm staying un-less you're going to a hotel with me. Which is it?"

His look broached no argument. She leaned her head back and closed her eyes. There was no point in arguing with him, he'd win. She was excit-ed to back on her own turf. For some reason it gave

her the security and stability to withstand his sensual assault.

All he had to do was look at her, and her
insides melted. His closeness in the confines of the
luxury car made her itch to touch him and feel his
lips.
She shook her head combatting her wayward
thoughts and inclinations. Santo was like a drug to
her system.

The car pulled alongside the curb before her
apartment complex. Maddie looked at the modest
exterior of her building and then the ostentatious
reality of his jet-set lifestyle. The two of them were
worlds apart. Her a humble, middle-class working
citizen. Santo a world class entrepreneur.

They stepped from the warmth of the car to
the bitter cold outside. Maddie shivered and without waiting for Santo she rushed inside. Walter, the
doorman, smiled widely and welcomed her back. He
nodded briskly to Santo before stepping aside.

Santo frowned when he saw the bland, modest interior. His snobbery was showing. Her lips
compressed together with annoyance. He had no
right to snub his nose at her home. It was what she
could afford. And in New York City you got what you
paid for.

Inside the apartment she looked around. Everything seemed to be in order. The place was small but clean and orderly. She adored her twice loved furnishings and shabby chic style.

Santo looked larger than life in the cramped surroundings, but he didn't seem to mind. His breathtaking face and lithe body caused a hitch to catch in her throat. His suave frame plastered against hers brought swirling memories crashing through her mind. A mere brush of his kissable mouth sent her world tilting.

Their luggage arrived, and he sat it inside the door.

Stepping away from the door he gave her a tempting smile. "Are you doing okay? Can I get you anything?"

She stepped around him and made her way to the small kitchen. The kitchen island becoming a barrier. "I'm fine," she promised. "Don't worry about me."

Not that she thought he would.

"Unfortunately, I must leave you to handle some prior engagements. I'll try to wrap things up quickly." His gaze flickered as he watched her fidgeting hands. "Don't wait up."

She watched his retreating back. "I won't."

He stopped briefly at the door his shoulders flexing, but he didn't turn around.

A whoosh of air flowed from her lungs. The released pressure calmed her frazzled nerves.

Maddie pulled a teakettle from the cupboard and filled it with water placing it on the stove. Removing a cup, she found some ginger tea bags. She placed Santo's suitcase at the end of the couch and took hers to the bedroom. She looked around at the downhome comforts that were so unlike Santo's. This was her reality, this was her life. Not the glamourous lifestyle he led.

The pot began to whistle. Filling the mug, she sat down on the couch and propped her feet beneath her.

She called her sister inviting her to come over. Colleen was older than Maddie, but they had always been close. Confidants. However, Maddie hadn't confided in her about her relationship with Santo lately. She hadn't told a single soul. What did she say? She didn't even know what her marriage was or wasn't. Her sister had gotten her through many tears when she'd left Santo last time. Colleen wouldn't be happy she had become caught under his spell again.

A rat-a-tat-tat at the door alerted Maddie to Collen's arrival. Flinging open the door tears streaked down her cheeks.

"Hey, sis. I've missed you," Colleen hugged her tightly after stepping inside the door.

Maddie's heart soared with happiness upon seeing her sister. "I've missed you," she said between huge sobs. "I'm so happy to be back home."

Collen pushed her back to arm's length and examined her tear stained face. "I know all of this isn't from missing me. So, what gives, Maddie?"

Maddie threw her a watery smile. "Is it that evident?"

Colleen laughed. "You never where good at keeping secrets. We've all been worried about you. Not that Santo isn't a good upstanding guy, but you haven't hardly called or anything."

She led Maddie over to the couch and patted the cushion beside her. "You look pale, sis." Colleen cast her a worried look. "Are you feeling okay? Have you lost weight?"

"I'm fine," she assured her. "Just tired. Could be the jet lag." She turned toward Collen and criss-crossed her legs in front of her.

"Maybe," Colleen said, doubt written upon her face. "Santo?" She looked about spotting his suitcase.

"He's gone." Maddie shrugged her shoulders.

"Some business stuff, but who knows. How's dad, mom, the family?"

"Everyone is fine," Colleen said. "You," she quizzed. "I swear you look really piqued. You sure you're feeling okay?"

Maddie wrinkled her nose. "I had a little dizzy spell on the plane earlier. Nothing serious. It passed pretty quickly."

Colleen cocker her head to the side and gave her an enquiring glance. "Is this the first time you've been dizzy?"

Maddie thought for a moment. "Yes."

"Anything else?" Colleen asked, her mind racing.

"What?" Maddie frowned. "Why are you looking at me like that?"

"When's the last time you had your cycle?" Maddie threw her a horror-stricken look. "No," she shook her head adamantly. "Not possible."

"So," Colleen rolled her eyes. "You haven't slept with Santo?"

Streaks of red coated Maddie's cheeks. She looked away. "I didn't say that."

"Exactly," her sister said sagely. She stood up. "You stay put, and I'll be right back. Isn't there a twenty-four-hour pharmacy close by?"

Maddie shook her head a dazed expression written all over her face. After Colleen left she sat frozen to the spot. Oh, my God. Oh, my God she chanted to herself. It couldn't be, but she knew the possibility was inevitable. Their sex had been unprotected. Unprotected sex produced pregnancies. It wasn't like she wasn't old enough to figure that out. Santo had never asked, and she hadn't told him she wasn't on any contraceptives. She placed her hand upon her rumbling tummy. What she had wished for may now be present. A child. Santo's child.

Colleen returned with a white pharmacy sack in her hand. "Here," she said. "You get in the bathroom and take this test."

Maddie clasped her whitened knuckles around the bag and stared at it. She was scared. Fricking scared to find out. This would change the whole dynamics of their relationship. Santo wanted her pregnant. He wanted an heir.

She knew her sister, and she would not leave until she knew the results of this test. So, Maddie walked, what seemed like a mile, to the bathroom and shut the door.

She stared at the two red lines. Pregnant. She was pregnant. Maddie sat there on the toilet seat positive it couldn't be true. She couldn't be pregnant. Now, what the hell was she going to do?

There was a soft tap on the door. "Maddie? Maddie open the door. The doorknob turned back and forth, but she had locked it. "Madison Renee Adams open this door," her sister demanded.

Maddie sat there for a few more seconds, then she opened the door. Her life would never be the same. Children were precious cargo and demanded parent's complete devotion. When Colleen saw her face, she knew the answer. She took the wand from Maddie's lifeless fingers, looked at it, then threw it in the trash.

"Hey, snap out of it Maddie. So, your pregnant. It happens to the best of us." Colleen tried to ease the tension. "I have two ornery examples myself."

Maddie bit down on her lip nipping it sharply with her teeth. She was in shock. She had Santo's child growing inside of her. What would he say? Would he be happy now it had happened? How was she going to tell him? She shook her head. She couldn't, not yet.

Her sister led her out of the bathroom and sat her down on the couch. "I'll get you some water to drink. She quickly came back with a full glass.

"Well," Colleen said, "now what? This changes everything. You and Santo must work this out." Maddie sipped the water and stared blankly into space.   "Nonna said we had to produce an heir." She looked pleadingly at her sister. "We can't bring a child into our relationship. It's so messed up."

Colleen sat back down beside her and pulled her into a tight embrace. "What are you babbling about?"

"The Will," Maddie continued. "Santo's

grandmother left Casa de Barrella to me under one stipulation we had to produce an heir."

Colleen pulled back. "And if you didn't?"

Maddie shook her head again. "The villa went to the church and I..." She stopped and started again. "And we ended our farce of a marriage, and I'd never see Santo again."

Colleen looked at her, sisterly understanding written in her eyes. "Listen sis these things tend to work themselves out. You love him. Quit dancing around the issue and tell him the truth. He'll understand."

"What if he doesn't," Maddie cringed. Unhappiness and misery shadowing her pale, withdrawn face. "Then what? I use to love him, but I don't know anymore. I want to have faith and trust him, but I'm not the naïve, young girl I use to be."

"Exactly," Colleen said. "You're married, have a child on the way, work things out. Now come on," she held out her hand, "let's get you tucked into bed. You need your rest." She smiled sympathetically. "The first trimester is a bear." She laughed. "Don't you remember my pregnancies?"

Maddie smiled. "Yes, I remember. Don't remind me."

Maddie changed into her pajamas, brushed her teeth, and climbed into bed. Kissing her forehead Colleen reassured her everything would be alright.

Then she left.

Maddie laid there in the dark, her brain saturated with so many crazy thoughts and questions. Santo deserved the truth, but she was barely pregnant. She had time to make a plan. Decide how to approach the subject.

Tomorrow. Tonight, she'd sleep and tell him tomorrow.

She woke. Her breath caught within her throat. She was disoriented. Her eyes dimly focused on her surroundings. And then it registered. She was in New York, in her apartment, in her bed. Her neck was stiff. She formed a kink on the right side. She had a beginner's waltz of a nagging headache. She rolled her head in a circular motion releasing pressure from her neck. It popped.

Santo was in her bed. His massive frame silhouetted in the darkness. The evenness of his breathing indicated that he was sound asleep. She felt as if the weight of the world had been dropped onto her shoulders. Her pep talk, from earlier, completely vanished. She was right back where she'd started. She wondered when he'd came back, she hadn't heard him. She hadn't wanted him in her bed, but her apartment was a one bedroom. He hadn't been given a choice except to sleep on the couch. His tall frame would have been cramped.

She slipped out from between the covers and tiptoed toward the door.

"Maddie."

She halted. Santo's voice sliced through the darkness.

"Where you off to?" he asked, his voice sounded gravelly from sleep.

"I can't sleep," she said. "I thought I'd get something to drink."

He stood, she could see the outline of his shadowy figure in the dimness. Thank goodness he wasn't nude, he had on his boxer briefs.

"I'll come with you," he said moving toward her. "Sorry I was so late. You were sleeping so I didn't wake you."

Maddie slipped out the door and padded across the wooden floor. Flipping on the kitchen light she pulled a bottle of water from the fridge. She passed a bottle to Santo.

"Thanks." His hair was mussed from sleep, but he was still as sexy as hell. He'd pulled on some jeans, but he'd left the button undone. She stared too long not to be caught. Her eyes popped up when he cleared his throat. He smiled knowingly. Her brain malfunctioned. Her self-inflicted abstinence made her crave his touch.

All the earlier emotions came rushing back to

clutter her brain with doubt and indecisiveness.

Santo studied her pale, wan features. "Is everything okay?" His mouth compressed. "Nothing happened while I was gone? No more sickness?"

Her stomach muscles tightened. She had never been a good liar. Growing up her brother and sister always instructed her to run interference for them when they did something they weren't supposed to do. She would always cave when her parents put on the pressure. Spilling out all the horrid details. Finally, her siblings learned to tell her nothing.

Maddie sat on the sofa and pulled her knees up beneath her chin. "Everything is okay. My sister came over and we had a good visit."

He sat beside her, and she pushed back into the cushions keeping the distance between them. One brush of his touch and she'd crumble.

"How's your family?" He said ignoring her resistance. Yet, his grey eyes bore into hers.

She wanted to ward him off, but the small confines of her apartment presented no room for an escape.

She ran her tongue along her upper lip. "They are great," she assured him. "How long will we be here?" she asked. "I would love to see my parents and brother too."

He nodded. Taking a big swig of water and

emptying the plastic bottle. "Tomorrow. I have meetings in the morning, but I can meet you at your parents in the afternoon. If things go as planned we'll fly out the next day."

She'd prefer him to not show up at her parents, but it would be rude to deny him. She sighed. "If you're busy you don't need to come."

His eyes narrowed. "You don't want me there? Your family welcomed me once, won't they again?"

A furious light glinted from his stern glance. She'd upset him. "Yes. My family likes you Santo. They aren't the problem, I am. You know this."

His coiled muscles visibly relaxed. "Are you, mio caro?" He lifted a soft, curling tendril from her face and smoothed it back behind her ear. The wisp of his fingers against her skin made her shiver with awareness.

She exhaled, her cheeks filled with color, her pupils dilated. She pressed her cheek against his hand.

His head moved toward hers, she waited for his piercing kiss. Closing her eyes, she waited. And waited.

His lips grazed her forehead. Her eyes popped open, cloudy and confused. Longing for this man consumed her. Even though she should resist.

Santo abruptly released her and leaned back.

The want in her eyes sent red-hot shards of desire lancing through him. His hunger was nearly unbearable. Her skin was so soft, her mouth so pliable, it was taking all the will power he could muster not to ravage her.

Her chest heaved from frustration. Her breathing shallow. The throbbing hot ache of desire shot straight to his groin, making him hard all over.

Her sharp little sighs and short little breaths whetted his appetite. He wanted to delve his tongue between her lips and take them both on a sensuous journey to utter fulfillment.

Her breasts rose and fell beneath her top.

He gritted his teeth. He stood and moved away putting distance between them. He'd been labeled scrupulous in business but not in relationships. He wouldn't take advantage of her weakness, which was him. This he knew for sure.

She looked exhausted. She needed rest. So, did he.

Hurt filled her eyes.

She watched him move away. It was her own fault. She'd been pushing him away.

"Santo?"

A ghost of a smile lifted his lips. "You're tired, Maddie. I'm tired. We need rest."

She glared at him. "Don't tell me what I need.

I can make those decisions for myself."

She knew he wanted her, she could see the evidence.

But he still shook his head.

"Come to bed. To sleep," he said, giving her an I know best look. "But be assured, Maddie, that I want you. There's not a day that goes by my body doesn't crave the satisfaction that yours gives. But you need time," sincerity filled his eyes, "and I'll honor that. When you come back to my bed it will because you want to, you need to, and I will enjoy every minute."

She wanted to say something. Something that put the control back in her court. Her gaze shifted. Frustration filled her eyes. She wanted to ignore the promise his half naked body had on her. But for the life of her she couldn't figure him out. He was a brilliant tactician who'd turned his grandmother's strategy, with impossible odds, into a win-win situation for him.

Chapter 11

Her mother pulled her into a warm, welcoming hug as soon as she came through the door. Maddie's tearless days had ended. She cried about everything.

She was blaming it on hormonal imbalance.

"Oh, Maddie," her mom said as she looked at her rivulets of tear drops dampening her cheek. "Don't cry sweetheart. We're so glad to see you."

Maddie hiccupped trying to stop the flow of tears.

Her family were a rambunctious lot. Noisy, everyone talking at the same time, and endless teasing.

The house was full. Her brother, Cole and his family of five. Colleen with her husband and two little monsters she lovingly called nephews. Her dad and mom.

Suddenly the importance of commitment and family bore down on her. Could she be a good mom? Did she have what it took? Children required a total commitment. Her hand slid over her belly. Together they had created a life, and now she must protect this child with her life.

They were all congregated in the kitchen when the doorbell rang.

"I'll get it," Cole said striding to the door.

Maddie was sitting at the table with her nephews and nieces coloring when Santo entered the room. He was dressed in a dark blue Armani suit looking larger than life. She swallowed hard. His presence making her insides sizzle with awareness.

Although he was her husband, she still trembled when confronted with his glorious, handsome face.

Everyone in the room waited with bated breath for someone to say something. The stillness was deafening.

Her dad finally made the first move. He slapped Santo on the shoulder and shook his hand. "Welcome back, old boy. Good to see you again."

Santo nodded. Then his deep grey pools caught and held hers. Her nephew decided to take a crayon from her niece. Sadie let out a scream. Colleen reprimanded her son and the tension left the room. Noise abounded.

Santo came up behind her and placed his hand on her shoulder. She turned and he smiled.

"Looks like you're busy," he said. "Need help?"

Maddie laughed. "Yes," she said breathlessly. "I'd forgotten what a handful this brood can be."

After that the day sailed by with lots of laughter, food, and conversation. Her family accepted

Santo's presence as if he'd never been gone.

The guys had congregated into the living room watching a game. The kids all sprawled on the floor with some electronic device or another.
Maddie was helping her mom wash the dishes. Her mom kept giving her a questioning look. "What mom?"

Her mom smiled knowingly. She pointed at the plate in Maddie's hand. "You've dried that dish five times now. Do you want to tell me what's going on?"

"I don't know what you mean," Maddie said nonchalantly sitting the dish on the counter.

"I'm your mother. Something's troubling you Madison." She gave her a stern glance. "You've been eyeing Santo like he's a cup of chocolate." She smiled. "Don't get me wrong, a man like that was made to be noticed. Is everything okay?" Concern filled her voice.

"Yes," she started but then shook her head. "No. I'm scared. I want to trust him. I want to make our marriage work. But what if we can't? Then what?" Tears welled up in her eyes again. "I don't know what I want."

"Do you love him?" Her mom asked.

Maddie nodded her head. The words lodged within her throat.

"Then make it work," her mom said sincerely.

"When you love each other, the past must be forgotten. Now, you have a child to think about."

Maddie froze, nearly dropping the plate she was holding.

Her mom laughed. "Don't act so surprised. A mother knows these things. Trust me, I knew the moment you walked through the door with tears in your eyes."

Her mom took the plate from her lifeless fingers, setting it down, then pulled Maddie into her arms.

Maddie squeezed her mom. The darn tears began again. "Do you think Santo knows?" she whispered.

"No," she patted her back. "But you better find the right time to tell him. He deserves to know. Now go," she shoved her toward the living room. "Get plenty of rest and take care of yourself. We all love you, and we're only a phone call away."

It had never been so hard to leave home. She hugged them all, too many times to count, before Santo insisted they must go.

The limo was waiting outside on the drive. Maddie frowned. "Why didn't you call a cab? Do we always need to be, you know," she waved at the imposing vehicle, "so noticeable?"

After spending the day with her normal, middle class family, Santo's jet-set lifestyle seemed so over the top.

Santo chortled. His energetic laugh promising. "We have unlimited use of the car while we are here, so why not utilize it? Plus," he turned and looked at her, "it's more comfortable."

"True," she agreed smiling timidly. His sexy smile igniting instant heat.

They climbed into the warmth of the car. Silence surrounded them. She glanced at his profile, but he only stared out the window.

This man had broken her heart once before, could she risk allowing him to do it all over again?

• • •

She still hadn't told him. Her morning sickness was becoming more frequent. Her appetite had nearly vanished.

She was staying in her own room, and Santo had made no attempt to touch her. He'd been gone a lot working. She hadn't complained because she needed the time to formulate her thoughts and decide what to do. Her mom had made it sound so easy, but it wasn't.

She was lying beside the pool, wet from her recent swim, when his presence blocked the sun.

She pushed her sunglasses onto her head and

squinted at his towering figure.

He was shirtless in his swim trunks. She was always amazed at how good he looked.

"I thought I'd join you."

"Good," she said and smiled.

Santo dove into the pool and came up several feet away. She remembered he was an excellent swimmer, but then again he excelled at everything.

The Barrella family were from old money. They had been financially successful in commerce and trade for over a hundred years. But it was Santo that had brought their software company into the twenty-first century turning it into a billionaire's success. High society and world class money were second nature to a man of his intelligence and skill.

She watched him swim. His strong strokes bringing him back and forth several laps before he pulled onto the edge of the pool. He made swimming seem effortless his breathing had barely increased. Rivulets of water streamed down his toned and muscled back.

He picked up the towel and rubbed his wet hair before standing and coming back to where she sat on the lounger.

She shaded her eyes from the bright sunlight with her hand. A jolt of white-hot awareness zinged though her bloodstream. A man like Santo was nearly too much for her over-worked heart. It pumped furiously within her chest. Her blood pressure increased while her breathing became shallow.

He looked at her his belligerent jaw softening as if he, too, was remembering her beneath him.

"I'm sorry for leaving you alone so much," he said, "but business has been very taxing. I had to close on some very important transactions that required my undivided attention. I hope you didn't mind?"

She shrugged her shoulders. "I don't mind. One of the hazards of owning your own company." She stood up wrapping a towel around her slender waist. He watched her, a shot of awareness penetrated his eyes.

"Are you hungry?" He gave her a onceover then stopped at her face. "Have you lost weight?"

"Actually, I am hungry." She ignored his second question. Her big secret reveal was upon her, and she knew it.

"Come on," he held out his hand to her, "I'll ask Isabella to whip something up."

She followed him into the coolness of the villa. Her eyes narrowed to adjust to the darkness. She shivered goose bumps scuttling up and down her exposed arms and legs.

"Cold," he inquired his brow arching.

"A bit," she said rubbing her arms.

He veered into his office grabbing his jacket draped over the back of the chair and placed it around her shoulders. She clutched it tightly around her, smelling the essence of him rising from its folds.

He led her onto the terrace. Going back inside he briefly talked to Isabella before seating himself across from her. She removed the jacket the warmth of the sun once again soaking into her skin.

His hungry eyes landed on her heaving breasts beneath the modest swimsuit. They seemed to swell her protruding areolas, more sensitized and tender. The sensation of heaviness and tightness was present everywhere. She crossed her arms hiding them from his view.

Isabella brought a tray filled with salad, cheeses, and meats. She offered wine, but Maddie placed her hand on top of the glass. Asking for water.

The pregnancy discovery had changed things.

This child growing in her womb had become her main focus.

She'd protect it with her life.

She ate a good portion of the food hoping it didn't make her sick. Santo helped himself to a second glass of wine and then leaned back in his chair.

He took one long sip of the liquid then sat it down. His fingers steepled the tips tapping together. "Tell me," he said, a bite to his voice, "When were you going to tell me about the baby?"

Her eyes grew wide as she looked at him.

"Yes, my secretive little wife. I know." His fierce gaze held hers demanding an answer.

At least now it was in the open. She no longer had to suffer in silence. "How long have you known?"

He shrugged. "I suspected on the plane. But, hearing you in the bathroom each morning confirmed it."

She lowered her head. "I thought you were gone."

"When were you going to tell me? I have the right to know about my child." His brooding good looks hardened causing her to cringe.

"Our child," she specified. "It's our child. I was going to tell you.   I hadn't found the right time."

"Why?" he captured her evasive glance. "Wasn't the right time the minute you found out?" She pondered his question, then bolted upright. The quickness of her actions filled her with sudden light headedness. The color leached from her face. Santo was instantly by her side sitting her back down.

Maddie gulped several deep breaths until the feeling passed.

A worried expression covered his face. "Are you alright?"

"I'm fine," she said. I stood up too quickly."

"Tomorrow you're seeing a gynecologist."
He gave her another concerned look. "I'm worried about all this sickness."

"Truly, I'm fine, Santo. This sickness is normal for a lot of women. My sister experienced the same thing."

"Still, we must get you to the doctor."
She opened her mouth to speak.
"No, no arguments. Tomorrow."
Her hand slid over her middle. Soon her belly would begin to grow. And then reality would sink in. She stood again. He clasped her elbow steading her.

She threw him a peeved look. "Really, I'm fine, Santo. I need to use the restroom."

He stepped back and waved his hand giving her a sheepish smile. "Be my guest."

She made it up the stairs and closed the door. That was it. He wanted to know about the baby, but he handled it like business. His signature move. Everything was business. Of course, he wanted to protect his business investment. Why did she hurt inside? From the beginning he'd been up front and truthful. A baby just cinched the deal. Nonna had tried. She'd flung them together in such a way to force them to enter an agreement. Find happiness, forgiveness.

No one was to blame but her. She'd fallen in love with him again. No, she'd always been in love with him. She had never stopped.

But, he didn't love her. She knew this with certainty. Santo was incapable of reciprocating the feelings that tortured her. It would be harder for her to stay knowing he didn't care.

Maddie knew him better than anybody. She knew his smile, his thoughts, his reactions. And more than that, she knew every intimate detail of his body. She'd memorized every angle, every line, and every dangerous part of him. But she knew nothing about his heart. The one organ that remained cold and aloof, robbing her of what she wanted most. His love.

She felt like a walking zombie. Lifeless, her heart a mass of confusion. Torn between wanting to go and wanting to stay. Santo had stolen her ability to find happiness. When she'd left two years ago no man had measured up. Her heart had waxed cold. He'd robbed her of family, home, and joy. Work had been her life line.

Sure, she'd gone to dinner a few times with

Edward, but it'd been nothing but platonic friendship. He had wanted more, but she'd never considered it. Now she knew why, Santo still had her heart and soul. The man she'd married for all the right reasons.

She pulled out her phone and booked a one-way ticket to New York. Her aunt's home in the Hamptons, somewhere he'd never look. He didn't know about it. She'd designed the home, so her aunt had given her the key code. It was a peaceful place where she could wallow in sorrow. The old saying misery loved company was just not true, misery didn't want company.

She shed her swimsuit and climbed beneath the shower spray. Her tears intermingled with the flowing water and disappeared.

So, caught up in her own misery she didn't hear him stealthily enter the shower. When his hands cupped her full, tender breasts she nearly jumped from her skin. Her startled eyes clashed with his. She wanted to deny him, but she couldn't. It had been so long. So, long. One last time.

She craved him, what would it hurt.

His thumbs plucked at her sensitized nipples. She moaned with pleasure. His touch sent direct messages straight to her core.

Her husband was a master at seduction.

She gave him her heart.

Then they moved to the bedroom. She exploded beneath him time after time until they both lay spent and replete.

He pulled her into his embrace. Her head tucked beneath his chin.

She treasured this moment, this closeness because it would be their last. Santo placed his hand upon her stomach. The possessiveness was clearly apparent. She held completely still not moving a muscle. He would never forgive her for leaving. Not for her but for his child, his heir.

He watched her. His gaze intent and steady. She tried not to blink. Or give him any indication of her plan to escape, disappear. His hand remained on her tummy.

"I thought you were using some form of contraception," he told her looking deep into her forlorn eyes trying to read the thoughts buried within their depths.

"I've had no reason to," she said softly.

Satisfaction entered his eyes. "There has been no one else?"

A slush crept up her neck into her face. "No," she admitted grudgingly. "There was you and only you."

He smiled a devilishly handsome grin and

squeezed her tighter. He appreciated the fact she remained faithful to him, to his memory. A rarity. All his past relationships had been open relationships, arrangements. No questions asked, just sex. However, it had always been different with Maddie. She'd mattered. She'd caught his eye from the very beginning.

He touched the rapid pulse beating in her throat. She swallowed holding the seriousness of his look. "What? Why are you looking at me like that?"

Santo propped up on an elbow the sheets sliding off his gleaming chest. "I don't know," he said. "You look different somehow, so fragile. Glowing. Does pregnancy do that to you?"

Spots of color rested high on her cheekbones. She blinked. She wasn't sure how to deal with this gentle side he was suddenly transmitting. It made her uncomfortable.

"Maybe," she smiled timidly.

"It looks good on you," he tapped her nose smiling. "Tomorrow we'll have you checked out and make sure things are going okay. Get some sleep."

Unbelievably, as wired as she was, she drifted off to sleep.

Santo watched the steady rise and fall of her chest. The playing field had changed. Everything had changed. Now, she was carrying his child, his blood, his destiny.

He wanted to create a protective shield around her. Guard her with his life.

He closed his eyes, confident he had things under control. Because that's what he did, micro manage his life and the people in it.

Santo woke her the next morning. He was fully dressed and looked refreshed and confident. Her eyes narrowed and blinked against the bright sunlight streaming into the room. Her stomach felt a little queasy, but manageable.

She steeled herself for the upcoming day.

The moment she was going to leave him.

She pasted on a bright smile. Bravado her driving force. He left her to get dressed, and she almost weakened. Almost. She had to continue to convince herself this was the best solution. The only plausible solution.

He would understand.

She went with him to the city. Leaving her things behind. What fit into her purse was all she could manage. She said what she needed and did what she needed so not to raise any red flags. No excuses.

The doctor appointment went off without a hitch. Santo remained close by her side asking a million questions. Giving off the persona of a proud father-to-be.

The doctor patiently answered every question assuring them everything was on track.

The morning sickness was common and would soon pass. A normal pregnancy and delivery shouldn't be a problem.

Satisfied with the doctor's answers Santo shook his hand and guided Maddie out the door.

Her bravery began to slip when he smiled at her like a Cheshire cat.

He hailed a cab leaving her the car and driver to return to the villa. He gave her a peck on the forehead, then she watched him go. A huge knot formed in the pit of her stomach. This was it.
Her opportunity.

She informed Isabella's husband, Andre, to take her to the airport. His brow rose in surprise, but he asked no questions.

For which she was thankful.

Recollections from her rapid departure two years ago came crashing back. The pain was just as unbearable. She sat blood leaching from her face when they reached Peretola Airport. She opened the door and rushed from the car before she lost her nerve. She paused at the glass doors, hoping deep in her heart, that Santo would appear and sweep her into his arms and beg her to stay.

But, he didn't appear.

She boarded the plane her resolve strengthening. The vestibule was crowded. The flight would be long. Nothing like the luxury of Santo's private jet. Again, she clutched her middle. The baby that grew inside her was now her future. Her sole responsibility. She would give it all the love it deserved. Her child would become first. Her needs second.

She left the airport and rented a car. She safely reached her aunt's home. The long private driveway curved up to the luxury home. She let herself in. She'd called her aunt letting her know she was invading her vacation house. The urge to jump back on the plane and return immediately plagued her.

But she must let the past go.

Was she a fool for running away? Maybe.

She crawled onto the plush white sofa and stared out the bank of windows. The view of the beach was nothing short of spectacular.

But she felt empty inside. She hurt. Oh, how she hurt. Her eyes burned, she huddled into a ball, misery consuming her.

She cried like a baby.

Tears of sadness, tears of sorrow, and tears for a life that could never be. But the villa was intact. She wouldn't be responsible for that catastrophe. They'd produced an heir. His grandmother's requirements had been fulfilled. All the tiny little details could be dealt with later. Much later.

Chapter 12

Santo slammed his fist down on the desk. "What do you mean you dropped her off at the airport?" His furious grey eyes landed on Andre. Their depths boiling like the severest storm clouds.

Andre bowed his head shoulders slumped. "Sorry, signore. She demanded I take her. I couldn't deny her request."

"Go," he ordered, waving toward the door. "It's not your fault."

"Yes, signore." Andre exited quickly.

Santo felt empty. Betrayed.

It wasn't Andre's fault, it was his. His alone. He paced back and forth across the tiled floor. Agitation simmering uncontrollably beneath the surface. He'd let down his guard. He hadn't suspected a thing.

This time she'd taken a part of him with her. His child, his family.

They'd made such passionate love together. It had been different. Their closeness was so genuine. She'd been sending him an important message, and he'd been too blind to see it, recognize it. She had given him what he needed the most, her heart and soul.

But, still, she withheld her trust.

Trust. Only a five-letter word, but it carried so much impact. Without trust they were unable to move forward. His Nonna had spoken of trust and forgiveness, but he hadn't listened.

He was angry at her. He wanted to pound something and take his frustration out to relieve the pain. Pressure built behind his eyes. A single bead of moisture leaked from his eye. Santo swiped away the weakness.

"Dio," he cursed beneath his breath. He was crying. Men didn't cry. He sure as hell didn't cry. What was happening?

He missed her. He missed them. His child was a reality. The doctor's report had made it a reality.

He cared. My, God, he cared. More than he had ever admitted, even to himself. She had taken a part of his heart before, but this time, she had taken it all. He was paralyzed with fear that she would never come back. His stubborn pride had pushed her away. He'd lost her.

He was heartbroken.

His heart ached. His eyes burned. He was consumed with grief.

He got on the phone. He had to find her.

. . .

Maddie carried her sandals in one hand and a

bottle of water in the other as she walked along the water's edge. The waves crashed against the sand and over her feet. She'd been in The Hamptons for two days. The waterworks had been turned on because she'd cried for most of it.

The sun was shining bright, but it was chilly. The water was cold, but she didn't care. The cold was invigorating, keeping her blood pumping. Her hair was pulled up into a haphazard ponytail, her rolled up sweats were damp from the waves, and her nose was bright red from constant wiping.

She was an absolute mess. She didn't need to look in a mirror to know it. She was so lonely. It was unbearable.

Her heart ached.

It hurt so much. Oh, how it hurt. After all the pep-talks, all the denial, she's allowed Santo back into her heart. False hope and broken promises. She loved him without measure. A life without him in it seemed so meaningless. But, now, she had this baby. And even though it was newly forming it'd come to mean so much to her.

She rubbed her still flat stomach anxious for the moment it would begin to grow.
Was it a son or daughter?

It didn't matter as long as it was healthy. But she couldn't help but think of a little boy with black hair and steel grey eyes that mimicked his father's. A spitting image of his daddy. Or, a little girl, with dark hair and grey eyes. She knew the child would inherit Santo's dark good looks over her fair complexion and hazel eyes.

Waves of grief washed over her again causing her chest cavity to constrict.

She had endured this misery two years ago, but the pain seemed much worse.

Maddie sat down upon the sand. Wiggling her toes, she pushed them into the grainy granules. She stared out at the choppy water hoping and wishing he'd come looking for her. How could he? No one, except her aunt, knew her whereabouts. But, he hadn't before. Why would he this time?

Santo had a stone-cold heart.

She picked herself up off the sand and headed back toward the house. She couldn't stay here wallowing in self-pity forever. She had to go home. Pick up the pieces and get on with her life.

She had to forget him. She had their child to think about now. Of course, he'd be involved in their life. Santo would never shirk his duties. He'd take fatherhood very seriously as was his way.

Maybe in time, she'd be able to approach him without all this unbearable pain in her heart. People mended from broken hearts all the time. She could too.

She squinted into the glinting rays of the sun. There standing at the base of the wooden steps was a man. Her heart somersaulted within her chest.

Santo.

Every sexy, glorious inch of him was highlighted by the sparkling beams. His jacket was slung over his shoulder, his shirt unbuttoned exposing the V of his chest. His hair was tousled from the wind.

Maddie halted and stopped a foot from him. "How did you find me?"

"I called your phone. Why didn't you answer?" His eyes sparked their annoyance.

"I turned it off," she stated, not allowing his bold gaze to dampen her spirit. His face filled with sharp intensity, and something she couldn't quite identify.

"That was damn foolish of you," he stated accusingly. "I've been running all over New York, knocking on every family door, searching for you. Do you know what kind of fool that made me look like?"

She smiled before she could stop it. His eyes squinted, no humor in them. "No one would think you look a fool, Santo." Her heart pounded. She bit the corner of her lip. His murky eyes softened to instant desire.

"Don't do that," he voiced harshly, the sound rough and gravelly. "I can't think."

She let go but bit the other side. He groaned as if in misery. Her stomach muscles quivered. "What are you doing here? Why did you find me?"

He raked his fingers through his hand. The ends spiked. "Your mom thought you might be here." He frowned. "By the way," he continued, "they're all worried sick about you. They are upset you didn't call."

"It's only been a couple days." She tilted her head. "I would've checked in eventually."

"Don't do it again."

"What?"

"Leave." His dark pools bore laser sharp holes into her face.

"I had to," she said. "We were doomed from the start. "I'm sorry I snuck out like that, but I knew if I told you, you'd convince me to stay." Her lips tightened. "I want to get on with my life. Get on with yours." She started again. "We'll work out a joint custody agreement. Our child will know you. I won't keep it away."

He clasped her upper arms. "You're damn right I'll see this child. It's our child, Maddie, mine and yours. It needs both parents. Do you understand me? I will not have our child tossed back and forth between us."

"And I won't stay married to a man that doesn't love me. Child or not." Huge tears filled her eyes. "Just leave me alone."

He gently shook her. "I can't. Do you hear me. I can't live without you. I love you, Maddie. I always have. I was too stupid to accept it or realize it."

She shook her head. Disbelief written upon her face. She yanked away from him. "Don't lie to me, Santo. I can't take it. The damage has been done. Don't spout words of love and commitment when you don't mean it. You've always held a piece of yourself back a solid barrier surrounding your heart."

"It's the truth, Maddie. The honest truth. I love you, very much." His strong jaw flexed and tightened.

"It's just about the sex," she clasped her middle, "and now our child." Emotion thickened her voice. "If you loved me why didn't you come and tell me before? I died inside waiting for your call, for a text, anything, but nothing. Absolutely nothing."

"I did come," he whispered.

Her eyes flew up to meet his. "When?"

"When you left before," he said, wrapping his jacket around her shoulders when she began to shiver. She stuck her arms in the sleeves and accepted its warmth. "I came to New York."

"I don't understand."

"I saw you with Edward Wakefield." Her hazel eyes darkened. "Standing outside your apartment building," he added curtly. "He kissed you," she started to speak, but he pressed his finger against her lips. "Not on the cheek, not on the forehead, but on the lips. "It tore me apart. I wanted to rush over and rip him to pieces. You were my wife. My world."

Her eyes pleaded with his. "It meant nothing to me. Edward never meant nothing to me. Not like that. He's only a colleague, a friend."

"I know that now, but I didn't then." Her pulse pounded in her throat. "I wished I'd known. We've lost so much time."

He nodded his fingers brushing her cheek. "I want you, Maddie, and only you. Please say you'll come back. I know we can make this work."

She tried to breathe. She tried to think. Her tears fell freely, and he caught them with his fingertips, then his lips.

His tenderness nearly her undoing.

"I love you, tesoro." He held her hands the ice-cold fingers stiff within his grip. He rubbed blood back into their tips. "I thought I had stopped

loving you. I forced myself to channel out your memory, and then you were back." He held her teary eyes with the grey softness of his. "I wanted to make you hurt for hurting me. I wanted you to go but stay. I was so confused about seeing you again. I wanted to ignore the instantaneous desire swirling through me."
He looked at her. She just stared.

"Please, Maddie, say something, anything. Tell me to go. I will." His jaw twitched. His eyes hinted at sorrow. "I'll do anything you want."

She closed her eyes, then opened them again. "I'm sorry," she said simply.

Santo looked tortured. He dropped her hands and nodded. "That's it then," he said. The banging in his chest felt like a jackhammer. He tried love twice with the same results. It wasn't worth it. He was done. He decided right then and there he would never let another woman claim his heart. The pain was too much. Destructive.

He couldn't think or breath, but he turned and bounded up the wooden steps. The pain was con-suming him. He saw nothing but red. He'd laid his heart on the line, and she'd rejected him. The word rejection was taboo. Not part of his vocabulary. A man with his status, his position, wasn't often sub-jected to it.

Pressure built behind his eyes. The damn

threat of tears was near the surface. He coughed, blinking several times to prevent them. Agony clenched his gut.

"Dio," he muttered out loud. The ring. It was still in his jacket pocket. The one he'd wrapped around Maggie's shivering form.

He must retrieve the ring. His grandmother's ring. A family heirloom. He'd placed it on her finger so long ago. For better or worse, till death do us part. She had left it when she'd gone. Lying there beside the bed. A symbol of promises that he had broken.

When he turned the wind caught him sending cold shivers flying upon his skin. So, this was how it felt to be broken hearted again? He knew he would never recover.

But Maddie was there her ponytail flying in the wind. Wariness in her red and swollen eyes. "Santo."
She flung herself into his arms.

He held her, squeezed her, feeling her racking sobs.

"Hush, Maddie. Don't cry. You'll make yourself sick and harm the baby."

She stepped back and looked at him. Swallowing she nodded. "I'm sorry," he started to speak, but she held up her hand. "No, let me say this. I'm sorry I left you. The first time and the last. I didn't trust you. Trust is so important in a marriage. A home without trust, and honesty is broken. I couldn't stand the thought of raising our child in a home where that's lacking. So, I ran. I ran from you. I ran from me, but you can't run away from yourself. It goes with you. I thought you had never loved or would love me. When you said you loved me, I was in shock. Absolute shock. I'm not a coward." She straightened her spine brushing tendrils of hair from her face. "However, I've been acting like one. I told you before that I wanted you, and I still do. But not just your body, Santo, I want your heart." She tapped him on the chest. "I want all you can give, plus more. I loved you when I first laid eyes upon you. I loved you when I left. I loved you when I was gone and I love you now."

Heat filled his eyes. A tenderness painted with love.
True love. Everlasting love.

"I'm your wife. I'm going to remain your wife. I'm done running. I'm turning in my running shoes." She handed him her sandals.

She cocked her head and gave him a timid smile.

He clasped her arms and pulled her against him, and in raspy, low voice he said, "If you're planning on running away from me again," he smiled rakishly, "you'd better get some better damn running shoes." He threw the flimsy sandals into the sand.

She laughed. A genuine, heartfelt laugh that radiated around them.

The mistrust, the doubt, the fear, and sorrow suddenly disappeared. Poof, was gone.

She held his face within her hands, happiness filling her eyes. The agony that had crushed her chest was lifted. She hauled his mouth down onto hers and kissed him. I mean really kissed him. All the years of pent up frustration dissolved with that one kiss. It sealed their future. She pulled back her breathing ragged and shallow. His ragged and rough.

Intensity filled his voice. "I'm sorry, Maddie. I'm sorry for not taking you home a long time ago. For allowing my stubborn pride to get in the way of happiness. Will you forgive me?"

He dropped a kiss on the tip of her nose.

"Oh, Santo," she threw her arms around his neck. "We've been so stupid. So, stupid." Her eyes glinted with joy. "And you, my sweet, sexy Italian, you are the love of my life. My husband, my friend, my soul mate. And you're stuck with me. Forever and ever."

"Forever," he agreed. "There is nowhere else I'd rather be but, in your arms, my beautiful, little runaway minx. You're stuck with me."

He let her go and knelt down before her. Her

breath hissed in her throat. His hand reached into the jacket pocket and pulled out the ring box. "This is for you," he said, satisfaction lacing his voice. He opened the lid and his grandmother's diamond ring encircled with topaz sparkled in the dark velvet box.

Maddie gulped. Her eyes filled with watery tears.

He lifted the ring from the case and placed it back on her finger. "Now, it's back where it belongs," satisfaction entered the depths of his eyes. "I choose you Madison Renee Barrella, to be my wife, the mother of my children, and the light of my life. Will you be my wife, till death do us part, forever and ever?"

"Oh, yes, yes, and double yes," she said between laughter and tears.

He stood then. "So, then I pronounce us husband and wife. I may now kiss my bride."

And he kissed her.

Epilogue

Their boisterous little boy scampered across the green lawn. His wobbling legs reminded Maddie of a fledgling newborn colt.

Lukas Adam Barrella was thirteen months old and into everything. Maddie jumped from her spot on the grass when he tumbled headfirst. He released a healthy cry as she scooped him into the cradle of her arms. Her heartbeat palpitating with concern. She worried endlessly about her handsome little boy. Lukas giggled melting her heart with his luminous grey eyes. The image of his doting papa.

Speaking of him, Santo came strolling across the wide expanse of green lawn toward them. He tousled the baby's dark hair. Lukas extended his chubby arms. His proud papa lifted him against his chest.

"Papa, papa," he said sweetly.

Santo smiled, love filling his heart. Holding his son protectively against him, his voice thick with emotion. "Hello, my son."

Santo was an exemplary father. He adored his wife and it showed. Maddie's family travelled to Italy whenever their schedules allowed, and Lukas adored his cousins.

Maddie looked up into her husband's shimmering, proud eyes. Lukas was spoiled beyond belief.

They couldn't help themselves. "He is a charmer," she smiled sweetly at two of the most important men in her life.

"Like his mother," responded her husband softly, pulling her against him, brushing his lips against her moist lips.

A lot had happened since that wind-swept day on the beach in the Hamptons. They had flown back home and renewed their vows before family and friends. She had been very pregnant and glowed with happiness. Maddie's family had been ecstatic about their reconciliation. Her mother couldn't praise Santo enough.

Marco had gone into treatment. He and Vanessa had split and divorced. He was now dating a wonderful woman. Her and Maddie had become fast friends. Marco shared joint custody of Matteo, and Maddie discarded any thoughts he could have been Santo's child.

After the initial morning sickness her pregnancy and delivery had gone smoothly. Lukas had been born less than a year after Nonna's shocking stipulations. Casa de Barrella was now their family home. She knew Santo's grandmother was smiling down on them.

Right now, Maddie was content to stay home and spend every waking moment with their precious son. She'd resigned from her job, sold her apartment, and flown home to Italy. She was one hundred percent content. She valued her life here. The perfect simplicity and peacefulness of the countryside was integral to their life. No matter where they travelled, they were always glad to be home. Nonna had always known. She legitimately belonged.

Santo delegated some of his duties to his new CEO, Marco, relieving him of some of his international travels. He was content to stay home with his wife and son. There was not a day that passed by that Santo didn't assure her of his love and devotion. She basked in his love and praises. She couldn't hear him say it enough. All the bumpy roads they had travelled were now smooth.

Santo pressed a kiss on top of her head and held her close. Their son squirmed demanding release. He told and showed her frequently how much he loved her making every day count. Their self-inflicted separation was long forgotten.

The glaring sun spread warmth upon her skin and contentment filled her. Their happiness this past year made up for the past. Oh, so much. She was thankful every day for the blessings she'd been given.

Tears misted Maddie's eyes as she watched Santo, so lovingly, handle their son. He placed him on the ground and laughed when he tried to run. He looked into her eyes, the connection so strong and binding that she could barely breathe. She fluttered her eyelashes at him. His glinted with instant awareness. The spark sure hadn't died. It was as strong as ever.

He held out his hand and intertwined their fingers. "Are you ready?" he asked, stopping their wayward son.

She nodded, and they walked to the waiting car. They buckled little Lukas in his seat. The drive was short to the little chapel sitting on top of the hill. They walked, each holding little Lukas chubby hand, to the cemetery lying on the knoll. The bouquets of flowers were tucked in the bag hanging on Maddie's shoulder.

They stopped at the four graves that housed Santo's family. Maddie watched her beloved husband's face as he knelt upon one knee and pulled some weeds that crowded the space. He placed the flowers on each grave. His expression reflected the sorrow and grief he bore from the loss of his loved ones. She'd never known his grandfather, or his parents, but Nonna had meant so much to her. Yet, she suffered their loss because it hurt Santo so greatly. His hurt became hers.

"These are your grandparents," he told Lukas. The toddler stopped and listened. "I don't want you to be an only child," he continued, "because if your mama and papa aren't there I want you to have each other."

Lukas tugged on his papa's ear and smiled accepting what he was being told.

Maddie squeezed his shoulder and smiled. She hadn't told him, but his wish was already beginning to unfold.

Santo looked up. She smiled again, a glimmer of promise shimmered within her eyes. "Lukas doesn't have long to wait," she said, happiness shining upon her face. "I'm pregnant."

Santo smiled. Then he grinned. Then he leapt up and pulled her into his arms while Lukas sat at their feet. "How? When?" The words rushed out in quick succession.

"The doctor confirmed it today. In eight months Lukas is going to have a baby brother or sister."

Santo kissed her then. Laughed, then kissed her again. "Is it too soon?" he said worriedly. He pulled back and looked at her lovely face. "Are you ill?"

She patted his cheek. "So far it's been good. I feel fine."

He turned back to the graves. "Did you hear that?" he asked. "I'm going to be a papa again."

Santo smiled. Who would have thought he

would find total happiness, everything he ever wanted, but was too bullheaded to realize? His rapid family expansion made him complete. True contentment
filled him.

He held his beautiful wife. "Thank you," he
said wondrously. "I love you Maddie more than you
could possibly know."

And she smiled even wider and bit the corner
of her luscious lip.

He groaned. The fever burned even brighter
within the murkiness of his grey depths. He placed
a fiery kiss on the palm of her hand. Promising the
fire, she found every time she came to his bed.

They'd found forgiveness. The one thing Nonna had known they would find in each other's arms.

The End

Powder River Publishing
www.powderriverpublishing.com

About the Author

Lorine Gray's love of romance, reading and writing, was first inspired by authors like Janet Dailey, Johanna Lindsey and many others. Although, her first attempt at romance novel writing never saw the light of day, her passion for writing endured. She spends her days-and nights-dreaming up steamy alpha heroes and the strong-independent heroines that tame them. Other than writing, Lorine has a passion for restoring and flipping houses, traveling and spending time on the beach. She is the wife of a born and bred Nebraska rancher and mother of two wonderful children. She has also been blessed with four awesome grandkids who she loves spending all her spare time.